D1445094

IN THE SHADE OF THE CHESTNUT TREE

IN THE SHADE OF

Translated from the Hebrew by REUBEN BEN-JOSEPH

Illustrated by RICHARD SIGBERMAN

BENJAMIN TENE

THE CHESTNUT TREE

THE JEWISH PUBLICATION SOCIETY OF AMERICA

5741 / 1981 Philadelphia

Copyright © 1981 by The Jewish Publication Society of America
First English edition   All rights reserved
This book was originally published in Hebrew by
Sifriyat Poalim, Tel Aviv, copyright © 1973
Manufactured in the United States of America

Designed by Adrianne Onderdonk Dudden

Library of Congress Cataloging in Publication Data
Tene, Benjamin, 1914–
In the shade of the chestnut tree.
Translation of Be-tsilo shel 'ets ha-'armon. Summary: A memoir of
the author's childhood in Poland before World War II. Contents:
The carousel.—The trumpet.—The greatest prank.—Concerning
cats, a photographer, and Grandma Leah.—The pest. [etc.] 1. Tene,
Benjamin, 1914– —Biography—Youth—Juvenile literature. 2.
Authors, Hebrew—Biography—Juvenile literature. [1. Tene,
Benjamin, 1914– 2. Jews in Poland] I. Sigberman, Richard. II. Title.
PJ5053.T43Z46213   892.4'85'09 [B] [92] 80-22219
ISBN 0-8276-0186-7

CONTENTS

I passed my childhood in Warsaw, the capital of Poland. Our house was in the Jewish quarter, where the streets were always busy. We children used to play in the yard. There was a chestnut tree there that spread its green boughs above us and listened to our boisterous laughter. It was to the chestnut tree we came when we were sad as well. We clung to its trunk, weeping in its shade. When I grew up I left Warsaw and emigrated to Israel.

In time a terrible war broke out, and the city of my childhood was conquered by the Germans. Its Jewish inhabitants were locked up in the Ghetto, tortured, and deported to death camps. When the war was over, I went back to visit my city. I wanted to see its streets again, and my home. I missed the scenes of my distant childhood. I hoped to find my former playmates, my friends.

I looked in vain. Only ruins remained of the Jewish quarter. I walked for many hours in the Ghetto waste, searching for remnants. I found neither my street nor my home.

Then, all at once, amidst the wreckage, I saw a solitary tree. Its bark was split, its trunk scorched and scarred, and its upper branches gone. Even so I recognized it. This was my chestnut tree!

I sat down beneath the tree. It was spring, and the sun's rays glistened on its broken limbs. My eyes wandered about the ruins. There was a green park on the horizon, with the silver water of a lake among its trees. Seeing it, I was bathed in waves of memory. There, in the park, we used to play scouts. There, on the lake, I embarked with Sevek on our search for a desert island. Remembering Sevek brought back the whole gang: Shimek and Kubah, Edek and Moti, Estusha and Ulah, speaking to me as then, as then.

The chestnut tree was silent. I raised my head and couldn't believe my eyes. There were green sprouts on the black bark. The charred stump was blooming. The old, afflicted tree had come alive again in new youth.

It was then I decided to tell about that childhood of ours. Our exploits of long ago. Our laughter and our tears. A story about a group of Jewish children in a strange, alien world.

IN THE SHADE OF THE CHESTNUT TREE

THE CAROUSEL

It was a sunbeam fluttering over my face that woke me up. I opened my eyes and looked out the window. A spotless sky, the latest handiwork of the Creator, gave me a smile of pure, lucid azure. The top of the chestnut tree, the only tree growing in our yard, gleamed with green leaves. Among its branches voices rose in chorus, a morning prayer of birds. For a little while I lay there, listening to the merry chirps and aware that my own heart was beating happily too, as if I'd heard good news. While I was still wondering about the cause of my joy, I remembered: the carousel!

There was a carousel in the plaza, on the other side of the city park fence. This plaza, paved with round stones, was used for various entertainments. On Sundays, at twilight, the members of the firemen's band took their places there, playing gay marches that reverberated throughout the park. Any circus that happened to be in town would pitch its huge tent in the plaza. And now, for the past week, the carousel was spinning around there and drawing large crowds.

We children used to go to the plaza every day, gazing at the marvelous carousel. In the middle of it, fixed in the ground like the trunk of an ancient oak, was its central column, a round, wooden shaft; from its hub thick poles stretched out like a fan of branches, linked to little purple chariots and brown painted horses with gilded saddles. Every chariot had its own horse. At the top of the carousel, on the tip of the central pole, there was a round, wooden structure, in the shape of a dovecote, with an iron ladder reaching from the ground to its door.

We would stand there for hours, following the whirl of the carousel with our eyes. Piotr, the owner of the carousel, a gigantic Pole with a broad leather belt wrapped about his fat belly, sold the tickets: eighty cents for a ride on a horse, sixty cents for a chariot. His son, Yuzek, a full-grown, curly-haired fellow, stood to one side, hugging a hurdy-gurdy to his chest, its solitary wooden leg propped on the ground. When the chariots were full and all the horses had riders, Piotr winked at his son and Yuzek began winding the crank of the hurdy-gurdy, whose innards emitted gay, croaky melodies. At once the horses and chariots were off. Slowly at first, hesitantly, but then the rhythm quickened into a dizzy flight. No one knew if the horses were chasing the chariots or, with their eyes flashing, were fleeing in alarm from them. All those riding the carousel cheered loudly, the girls' braids flying playfully and the hurdy-gurdy grinding, as we looked on and on with longing eyes.

We children were poor. We never had enough to pay sixty cents for a chariot, and surely not eighty cents for a horse.

One evening my friend Shimek the redhead rushed over to my house and cried out from the doorway in a great voice, "Tomorrow we're going to ride the horses!"

"How? Did you find a fortune?" I asked.

"We don't need money," Shimek replied. "I talked with Piotr. It seems the carousel doesn't run by electricity. It runs by hand. Piotr told me to come early tomorrow morning and help run it. If I do a good job, at noon he'll give me a free ride on a horse. You can join me!"

My heart leaped with joy. Tomorrow my dream would come

true. I would sit in a gilded saddle, take up the reins of a brown horse, and gallop away!

The next day, as I lay in bed and felt my heart beating happily, I remembered Shimek's visit and understood the reason for my joy: the carousel!

I sprang out of bed, ate quickly standing up, and dashed out to the street. Running, I bumped into Shimek, who was coming my way. As we approached the plaza beyond the park, we could hear the croaky sound of the hurdy-gurdy and the cheers of those whirling on the carousel.

It was a lovely summer day, a fresh, clear morning. A lively breeze caressed our faces. The sunlight sparkled in the windows of the houses around the plaza, and the panes shone like gold. The purple chariots and gilded saddles dazzled us. The brown steeds galloped in a ring; it seemed their red nostrils were quivering. In one of the chariots a girl stood, gripping the pole overhead, and her skirt billowed like a bell in the wind.

We stood there, hesitating. When the carousel stopped, we plucked up our courage and went over to Piotr.

"We've come to work," said Shimek.

Piotr gestured toward the iron ladder propped on the "dove-cote."

"Go on up," he said, "but remember, you have to push with all your might. Don't hold back. If you cheat, it'll go hard with you! I won't let you ride the horses, and I won't spare the rod on you either."

To tell the truth, the rod didn't frighten us as much as the threat to deny us the privilege of riding.

"We'll work, you'll see!" Shimek cried, and we both dashed over to the ladder.

Entering the "dovecote," we had the feeling we'd stumbled into a dark, shadowy tunnel. It was round, built about the central column of the carousel, its walls made of wood with no window; only overhead, where the boards were fastened to the column, a pale light broke in. It was stifling in the "dovecote." The stench jolted us.

For a minute we couldn't make out what was going on around us. Once our eyes became used to the dark, we discovered a gigantic wooden wheel, set with spokes, encircling the round column. Between the spokes boys stood, wiping the sweat off their pale faces. While we wondered at the sight, the sounds of the hurdy-gurdy rose outside, and Piotr's voice was heard yelling, "Let's go!"

The boys pointed to the spokes. Shimek and I took the hint and slipped in between them. At once the boys started going around in a ring, each pushing his spoke—slowly at first, as if marching in place, but then increasing their speed, running around in a ring and cheering on one another loudly. Shimek and I pushed the spokes in front of us and raced around. If we stopped for a moment, the spokes behind us would have smashed into us and thrown us down. If we fell, the running boys would have trampled us.

Now we understood. It was this wheel, turning under the power of the running boys' muscles, that drove the carousel. There, down below, the horse riders and charioteers were delighted by their pleasant spin; here, in the "dovecote," the boys labored like galley slaves of old.

I ran around, straining to push the spoke with my hands and chest while my head grew dizzy. I felt I couldn't keep up with this wild race—in another minute I'd collapse. Then all at once the hurdy-gurdy was silent, and the boys let go of the spokes. For a moment or two they kept on running in the wooden wheel, until it slowed to a halt. One "ride" had come to an end.

We sat down, wiping the sweat that streamed from our foreheads. My throat was parched with thirst. Oh, for a glass of water, just a sip!

Through a crack in the floor I saw what was happening in the

plaza. The riders had got off the chariots and horses. Piotr was selling tickets to the crowd. While I was still stooping, pressing my mouth to the crack for a breath of fresh air, the hurdy-gurdy rang out again and Piotr yelled, "Let's go!"

Once again we were racing in a ring, pushing the spokes. I turned around and glanced at Shimek, who was running behind me. His breath spurted out in a harsh shriek. I was breathing loudly too.

The carousel stopped many times. It started off again many times. I felt my strength was failing and cursed the minute I'd listened to Shimek's proposal. Two hours passed, then three. In one of the breaks, when the carousel stopped, I decided to give up. Who was to prevent me? I was free, I could climb down the iron ladder and go back home. Just then I remembered the brown horse with the gilded saddle. A little more, another few turns, and I'd be on that horse, holding its reins! No, it couldn't be that all my labor was for nothing, the pain in my hands and chest, the stinging sweat, my dizzy head, the black circles dancing before my eyes!

While I was still struggling with myself, wavering, I heard Shimek's voice, low and ashamed: "I'm going." His freckled face was pale as a sheet. His lips quivered.

I wanted to join him, but some hidden power, stronger than me, held me in place. No, I wouldn't give up my appointed horse! So I quietly nodded to him and turned away, afraid of meeting his eyes.

Shimek climbed down. I kept up my hard labor, digging my feet into the wooden floor, pushing the spoke with my hands and chest, panting. I didn't know whether it was sweat or tears blinding my eyes.

Finally, when the carousel stopped, Piotr's head appeared in the entrance to the "dovecote." He beckoned to me and said, "That's enough! Go down and pick yourself a horse."

I went over to the door, my knees wobbling. A gust of fresh air hit me in the face. My legs faltered as I descended the ladder. Gripping the rungs, my hands trembled.

I stood by the carousel. Chariots painted purple. Brown horses with gilded saddles. I'd won! I had the right to pick any horse I liked!

I was about to go up to one of them when, at that very minute, I was dazed, overcome by nausea. I managed to leap aside, over to the park fence. I grasped an iron pole with both hands, bent my head, and vomited.

I felt terribly weak. I walked a few paces and sat down on the ground. The houses lining the plaza circled before me dizzily. Even the earth beneath me was in motion, spinning in a ring, rising and sinking all at once as if it had fallen into an abyss. I put out my arms, trying to hold on.

After an hour or so, I got up and went over to the carousel, which had stopped. The riders, their faces flushed, jumped down from the chariots and horses. Boys and girls and little children took their places, tickets in hand. There were still a few vacant horses. I went up to one of them and stood beside it. Never had I been so close to my heart's desire.

All at once I was looking at a crude horse made of cracked wood, its paint faded and its saddle worn. Its red nostrils now seemed to be bleeding. Its gaping mouth looked as if it were laughing, mocking me. And I—my legs were shaking. My eyes were full of mist, and hammers banged in my head: *boom boom boom boom!*

I knew then that I'd been wrong to come here. My beautiful dream had melted away. No, I wouldn't ride the horse. I wouldn't have the strength to mount it. And when it galloped, I'd only vomit again. And anyway, how could this worn-out, faded horse have enchanted me?

Slowly I moved away from the carousel. I left the plaza with its noise and clamor and, tottering, made my way back home.

The sky, blue when I came to the plaza, now grew cloudy. In the middle of the clear, sunny day, evening fell. The house windows that had sparkled like gold in the morning regarded me with dull eyes. And now the rain came. The heavens were weeping.

I walked down the street. I was crying mutely inside. My face was wet. I didn't know whether it was my tears or the raindrops.

THE TRUMPET

Sevek came over as I was doing my arithmetic lessons, preparing for the test that was to be given the next day. Since it was unusual for him to call on me in the evening, I looked at him with surprise. He bent over me and whispered in my ear, as if he had a secret to tell.

"Come on down to the yard!"

I wasn't eager to go along with him. I wanted to get ready for the test, and I was worried about my mother, who used to scold me every time I sneaked out after dark. But I had no choice. You couldn't say no to Sevek.

Sevek was twelve, two years older than the rest of us—Shimek, Kubah, Edek, and me. We five lived in the same yard, in a building on Nalevki Street, which was in the heart of Warsaw's Jewish quarter. Sevek was the first and foremost participant in our games and pranks and the final arbiter of our quarrels. His word was law.

When we reached the yard, which was wrapped in dusk, Sevek drew me over to the chestnut tree, the only tree growing in our yard. He put his hand into his shirt and pulled out something that sparkled. In the pale light emerging from the nearby window of a ground-floor apartment, I saw a toy, a little trumpet. I took it carefully in my hands, the way one takes a little bird, and I examined it well, from every angle.

The trumpet was made of a hornlike material. It was green all over with a gilded mouthpiece. A slender chain, also colored gold, was fastened to it from end to end. Never had I held such a lovely toy.

We boys of the yard had no toys. Our sisters played with rag dolls. Poverty-stricken, our parents never had the means to purchase toys. Perhaps they didn't feel the need to provide us with them. My father used to say to me, "A big boy like you—ten years old!—should be studying, not wasting his time on nonsense!" True, Shimek did have a rusty pocketknife, which he used to sharpen on the stones of the yard. Kubah had somehow come into possession of a whistle, and Edek had a broken spyglass, without lenses, which he'd found by a garbage container in the yard. Such was our entire treasure. But this didn't mean we never played.

First of all, there was football. Of course, we didn't have a real ball; we used an old sock filled with dirt. Somehow it was possible to kick it, but Heaven help whoever was hit on the head by that "ball"! It was an experience many had, with varied impressions: some claimed to have blacked out, some to have seen stars. There were other games, such as hide-and-seek. Sometimes we would climb up the chestnut tree—which became a mast, its upper branches a ship—and we would fancy ourselves sailing to distant lands. Edek would search the horizon with his spyglass. Shimek would grip his pocketknife, a pirate.

So we did have games of our own, but we never owned a real toy. It was no wonder I stood beside Sevek, holding the wondrous trumpet in rapture.

"Where did you get the money?" I asked.

"Who said I bought it?"

"Then how did you manage to get the trumpet?"

Instead of answering, Sevek took my hand and led me into the back yard. Our front yard was enclosed by shabby residential buildings; the back yard was lined with stockrooms. Sevek went up to one of the stockrooms and climbed the stairs at its entrance. His hand never let go of mine. Suddenly he stooped and put his hand in the wide crack between the doorsill and the heavy, wooden, iron-plated door.

"Stick your hand in!" Sevek commanded.

I did as he said. My hand groped along the concrete floor of the stockroom and came up against something smooth. I grabbed it and pulled it out.

My hand held a trumpet, a duplicate of Sevek's toy. I knew that the stockroom belonged to the owner of the toy store facing the street. One of the boxes in the stockroom must have broken, and the trumpets packed in it had fallen all over the floor. I stood still, holding the trumpet. My heart beat fast.

"You see, you don't need money!" cried Sevek teasingly.

"But the Bible says, 'Thou shalt not steal,' " I said in protest.

"I didn't come here to hear you recite the Ten Commandments!" snapped Sevek. "My pious friend, the Bible also says, 'Honor thy father and thy mother,' but how many times have I heard you get fresh and tell lies to your parents?"

Sevek raised his voice. I suspected that his outrage was meant to allay his own doubts. I stood there bewildered, the shiny trumpet in my hand: a green trumpet, with a gilded mouthpiece and a slender, gold chain. My heart ached. I had never ventured to steal anything. Even now, I had yet to cross the line. One movement on my part and the toy would be back in place, and no one would know of my wrongdoing. In fact, I had already approached the crack, but the hand holding the trumpet seemed to have a will of its own, shrinking back. Just then I heard Sevek's voice, more quiet this time, controlled and enticing.

"Don't be silly! You'll never get another chance to have a trumpet like this. The stockroom is full of boxes, and there are hundreds of trumpets in them. What harm is it to the rich storekeeper if one or two trumpets are missing? He won't even notice!"

If I still had any doubts, Sevek's speech saved me from them. I stuck the trumpet in my shirt and dashed back home, without a word of thanks to Sevek.

"What are you doing, running around in the dark?" my mother asked.

"Sevek called me." I tried to hide my flushed face from her. Luckily, my mother was busy and did not notice my excitement.

I never went back to those arithmetic lessons. It wasn't the test that worried me, but the trumpet. How could I put it out of sight? I decided that until I could find a proper place, I'd stick it under my mattress. Once my parents were asleep, I'd try to think of a better hiding place.

I didn't touch my supper. "I'm not hungry," I told my mother.

"Maybe you're sick?" My mother felt my forehead. It was cool, so she relaxed. Actually, I was hungry, but because my throat felt choked I couldn't be near food. All the while I was thinking about the trumpet. Oh, how I longed to take it out from beneath the mattress, to blow it just once!

Finally the lights went out in the house. I went to bed. I lay in the dark with my eyes open, stroking the trumpet, hugging it, pressing my mouth to the gilded mouthpiece, delighting in the slender chain. I wanted to see it in all its glory, but I was afraid to turn on the light. In the end, my desire won. I got out of bed stealthily, my hands feeling about the stove. Finding the match-box, I took a match and lit it. The little flame was reflected in the shiny trumpet, and I feasted my eyes on it. I only let go of the match when its flame reached my fingers and burned them.

The flame went out. I stood in the dark, my heart pounding. *I must hide the trumpet!* I repeated to myself. *Of course I'm sorry to part with it, but I can't leave it in a place where it might be discovered.* Suddenly I had an idea: the cupboard!

In our kitchen there was a large cupboard. The top shelf held the Passover tableware, which my mother used only one week a year. I found a chair in the dark and climbed up to the shelf. Standing on tiptoe, I stuck the trumpet in back of the polished copper pots that were lined up in a row.

I was satisfied. But back in bed, I lay awake a long time. I yearned to play with the trumpet again, and my heard ached since I was forced to part with it. At the same time my conscience bothered me. I couldn't fall asleep. It seemed to me that my father was standing by my bed. I could hear his voice, chiding and angry: "Thief!"

The next day, at school, I failed the test. It was impossible for me to concentrate on arithmetic. Thoughts of the trumpet filled my mind. Returning home, I ran to take it from its hiding place. But I couldn't. My mother never left the house for a minute.

Once it was dark, a strange restlessness gripped me. In my mind's eye I saw the stockroom in the back yard and the wide crack between the doorsill and the iron-plated door. Why, it was wide enough for me to put in my hand and get another trumpet! The stockroom was full of boxes, and there were hundreds of trumpets in them. Yes, Sevek was right. It was no harm to the rich storekeeper!

Deep in my heart I knew I shouldn't do it, but I was caught up in a strange fever that throttled the voice of wisdom. I was seized with greed. The crack in the stockroom door fascinated me, drawing me toward it. In the evening I stole out of the house and made for the stockroom. I stood there briefly in the dark, staring and listening closely. There was no one around.

I bent down at the stockroom door, and an instant later I straightened up and stuck a trumpet into my shirt. I dashed back home, but before I reached the stairs I noticed Shimek sneaking out to the back yard. Seeing his furtive steps, I became suspicious. Could it be that Sevek had revealed his secret to Shimek too?

Another night of agitation was upon me. Again I was stroking

the trumpet, examining it by the light of a match and hiding it on the top shelf of the kitchen cupboard, behind the Passover tableware.

Now I had two trumpets, but I wasn't pleased. I couldn't play with them. It was impossible to blow them without revealing my secret. As the days passed, my distress grew keener. At night I would toss in my sleep and hear in my dreams that voice of anger at my bed: "Thief!"

One day, as I was playing in the yard, I suddenly heard the sound of a trumpet from the window of Kubah's apartment. *Ta-ta-ta!* The next day, as I sat in the dusk by the chestnut tree, I saw Edek darting out of the back yard, his shirt bulging.

There was no doubt about it. Sevek had told his secret to the whole gang! I wasn't the only offender, but there was no point trying to console myself with that. My two trumpets in back of the Passover tableware did nothing to make me happier. On the contrary, I was sad. Guilty feelings gnawed away at me.

One day I heard Sevek's whistle, the whistle we all recognized as a kind of command. At once I stopped what I was doing and went down to the yard.

The whole gang had assembled in the shade of the chestnut tree. Sevek and Shimek were sitting there, and Kubah and Edek. When I joined them, Sevek addressed us sadly.

"We're in a mess!"

We kept still. We didn't know what he meant. So Sevek told us.

"This morning I went to the toy store to buy a ribbon for my sister, and I heard the storekeeper tell one of his customers that there'd been a burglary in his stockroom. Actually, I'm amazed. There are only five of us. How did he happen to notice just five missing trumpets?"

My heart squirmed. I lowered my eyes and the words burst out of my strangled throat. "I've got two trumpets."

"And I lifted five," cried Edek.

"Four for me," said Kubah.

"And three for me," added Shimek.

Sevek, who was good at figures, screamed, "Fifteen trumpets! You dirty crooks!"

"You'd better be quiet," Shimek upbraided him. "You were the one who showed us how!"

Sevek bent his head. We sat there a long time, not uttering a sound. Then Sevek said, "Maybe I was wrong. How are we going to get out of this now? The storekeeper said he had reported the incident to the police."

"How are the police going to trace us?" asked Kubah. "Even if they search our homes, they won't find anything! I hid my four trumpets in the basement, at the bottom of the coal bin."

"Very smart!" cried Sevek. "Don't forget, the police have bloodhounds."

"That's ridiculous!" Shimek said. "They call in bloodhounds on a murder case, not for a few miserable trumpets!"

Sevek and Shimek argued, but I wasn't listening. I felt my flesh creep. In my mind's eye I saw a gigantic bloodhound breaking into our house and charging at me, its teeth bared. I wanted to say something, but I was trembling all over. My teeth chattered.

Sevek got up and gave us, his juniors, the concerned look of an elder brother.

"There's no other way," he said. "Tonight, at twelve o'clock sharp, we're going to put the trumpets back. Make sure you sneak out quietly."

That night I went to bed, but I never closed my eyes. Once the house was quiet and I was sure my parents were asleep, I climbed up to the cupboard shelf, removed the two trumpets, and went back to bed. I put them on the pillow by my head, and for hours I lay there hugging and stroking them. Then I noticed that the trumpets were wet. They were wet with my tears.

At midnight we met by the iron-plated stockroom door. Each of us stooped in turn and stuck his prize in the crack. Sevek, one trumpet; I, two; Shimek, three; Kubah, four; and Edek, five. When we were through, we stood in silence.

Finally Shimek spoke, his voice quivering. "I never had a toy. I was so happy with the trumpets, and now I have to part with them!"

"It was a dream," Kubah sighed.

Edek said nothing. He rested his head on the iron-plated door and cried loudly.

"Stop bawling," Sevek scolded him. "Tomorrow we'll play football."

"The sock's torn and the dirt spills out!" I reminded him.

"It doesn't matter," said Sevek. "There's no lack of dirt. And we can always find another old sock, without the threat of bloodhounds."

We stood a little while longer in the yard. I looked up at the cloudy sky, spread in a heavy heap above the square yard. Just then one of the clouds parted, and I saw a single, twinkling star. It seemed to be winking at me and smiling.

I returned home and slipped in the door. I went to bed, looking at the darkness. Little by little my eyes closed, and I sank into a deep sleep.

THE GREATEST PRANK

I had two uncles, Gedalyah and Nachum, but I liked only Nachum. I was attached to him and spent many hours in his company. More than once I skipped the games in the yard in order to be with him.

Both my uncles lived on the same street. Uncle Gedalyah, the elder, was a wealthy timber merchant and lived in a large, comfortable apartment with a view of the park across the street. Uncle Nachum, a poor man of no means, lived in the basement in the back yard of an old building. All he could see from his window were the legs of the tenants throwing their garbage into the big bin.

Uncle Gedalyah was a tall man with bushy eyebrows, a long, broad, carefully combed beard, and collars that were dazzlingly white. Childless and stingy, he held himself proudly, with a look on his face as if he were about to fly into a rage. He went darkly about his four rooms, one of which served as an office. There he received the lumber dealers and foresters who came a long way to see him.

Every time I visited him I was enthralled by his spacious living room. A sparkling crystal chandelier with many branches hung from the ceiling. The floor was covered with a thick carpet.

Shiny silver vessels peeked through the glass doors of the cabinet. In the corner, beneath the window, sprawled a stuffed German shepherd, gray and life-size, a gift to Uncle Gedalyah from one of the foresters. The dog's big teeth were bared, and his red tongue dangled from his open mouth. As a little boy I was frightened by the stuffed dog, afraid to go near it. It seemed that any minute it would jump up and sink its teeth into me. When I was older, I got even with it. When no one was looking I kicked it, pinched it, and took my revenge for the terror it had caused me as a child.

Aunt Chayah, Gedalyah's wife, was a red-faced woman with a tongue like a razor. She surpassed even her husband in stinginess. I was never so lucky as to receive a single gift from her. When I came to their house she would finger her apron, take out a squashed, crumbling cookie or a sticky piece of candy, and bellow, "Come on, have a treat!" In exchange I was forced to listen to the reproaches she generously bestowed upon me. "Why are your hands so filthy? Where's that button on your shirt? You forgot to wipe off your shoes! Now you've got the carpet all muddy!"

No wonder I stayed away from their house. I went there only when I had to, with my parents, to pay our respects on the Sabbath.

There was another reason for my reluctance to visit Uncle Gedalyah. At the entrance to his house I had to pass by Stefan the doorman's apartment. Stefan had a German shepherd (a live one, not stuffed!) named Rex. This dog was the image of Uncle Gedalyah's specimen. Of course Rex was chained to the gate, but every time I went by he let out a resentful bark. Everybody was afraid of Rex. Uncle Nachum, on his frequent calls at his brother's house, was the only one who made friends with the cranky German shepherd, bringing him an occasional bone from the butcher's nearby. Rex not only refrained from barking at him but wagged his tail and licked his hands as well. Uncle Gedalyah would look on and grumble, "Since when do Jews make friends with dogs?"

I stayed away from Uncle Gedalyah's house, but I never

missed a chance to drop in on Uncle Nachum. Day after day I used to slip out to his basement apartment, skipping down the wooden stairs. Aunt Devorah would greet me with a smile, offering me a slice of buttered black bread, which tasted to me like a royal feast.

I wasn't allured by Aunt Devorah's refreshments as much as by Uncle Nachum, who was very different from his older brother. Uncle Gedalyah was a wealthy man; Uncle Nachum was poor. Uncle Gedalyah was well dressed and tall, with a long, broad beard; Uncle Nachum was short, with a little beard at his chin, and he dressed poorly. Uncle Gedalyah was strict and had a terrible temper; Uncle Nachum was easygoing, with flashing eyes and a mischievous smile, seemingly winking a jestful invitation: Now here's a trick to play. Come on, lend me a hand!

Uncle Nachum had a joke or witty remark for every occasion, telling them in his hoarse voice and enjoying what he said with a hearty laugh. An eternal cigarette clung to the corner of his mouth; the smoke rings he breathed were works of art. As I watched him at his tricks, he would throw me one of his clever questions, such as, "How many ends does a stick have?"

"Two!" I answered.

"And half a stick?"

"One!" I loudly declared.

And then Uncle Nachum would rock with great, thundering laughter. How did that short body come by such a tremendous laugh? When he laughed it seemed the walls laughed too. The mirror hanging on the wall shook, and the reflected pieces of furniture swayed liked drunkards. I was amazed and bewildered. What did Uncle Nachum think was so funny? Just try asking Uncle Nachum! He laughed out of a compulsion to be playful. He was a big clown, a clown by nature. He had to play jokes, fooling people, as full of mischief as any kid.

One day I went along with Uncle Nachum, who planned to visit a friend of his. Before boarding the trolley car, he said, "If it's all the same to you, I'm going to make everyone on the trolley wipe his nose."

At first I didn't catch his meaning. I thought he was joking as usual. But the minute we got on the trolley my eyes popped. At the very sight of Uncle Nachum, all the passengers began wiping their noses, some with their hands and others with handkerchiefs they took from their pockets. I was breathless with amazement. Then, glancing at Uncle Nachum, I saw that his nose was dirty, blackened with soot!

I still didn't understand. It was only when we got off the trolley that Uncle Nachum stopped and burst into his thundering laugh. At last he broke off, took a breath, and said, "What did I tell you! They all wiped their noses!"

"But it was your nose that was dirty, not theirs!" I argued.

"Silly boy," Uncle Nachum replied. "You don't understand human nature. When they saw the soot on my nose they all thought, 'Since this fellow's nose is dirty and he hasn't noticed it, my nose may be dirty too. I'd better wipe it!' "

Every time I went out with Uncle Nachum, there was a surprise in store for me. Whenever his mischievous urge got the better of him, he would warn me to stand aside. One day, after I had stepped back a little, Uncle Nachum stood in the street, threw his head back, cupped his hand, and looked through it at the sky. At once someone stopped alongside him and asked, "What do you see up there, my good man?"

"A Zeppelin," replied my uncle without batting an eye.

"What do you mean, a Zeppelin?"

"A Graf—a count."

"A count that flies?"

"Haven't you heard? That's the blimp they named after that count, what's his name? Zeppelin!"

The man joined him, cupping his hand to look up at the sky. In a little while a whole flock of Jews had gathered, throwing their heads back and looking up. Then Uncle Nachum slipped out of the

crowd, took my hand, and went on. As soon as we had moved away from the crowd, he broke out in a great laugh, and I was caught up in it and laughed too.

One day someone who looked like Uncle Nachum passed me in the street. At first I wasn't sure whether it really was my uncle or not. True, he had the same short figure, the same little beard, and the same shabby coat, but this person wore dark glasses and held a cane, tapping along like a blind man.

"No, no doubt about it, it's Uncle Nachum," I finally decided. I stood aside nevertheless, not sure if I should approach him.

Soon enough someone came by, a kind fellow whose heart was moved to compassion by the blind man. He went up to Uncle Nachum, put his arm through his, and said, "Please let me help you. Where is it you want to go?"

With the utmost caution, stepping slowly, he conducted the "blind" man. His face beamed; this was his good deed for the day! I followed them, amazed at the sight.

Suddenly, in the street, a black cat ran by, springing out of one of the gates. At once Uncle Nachum discarded his merciful escort's arm and dashed off, chasing the cat and waving his cane. The man froze in his tracks, gaping, a picture of dumbfounded wonderment.

I ran after my uncle, who was running after the cat, which was fleeing for its life. I found him in one of the yards. The dark glasses bulged in his jacket pocket. Uncle Nachum looked at me in triumph, and suddenly that great, mischievous laugh of his burst out.

"Uncle," I said, "why did you do it?"

"Why do I play all those other tricks?" he answered with a question. "There's so little to be happy about in this world, it's enough to make you explode! In fact, sometimes I want to scream. It's just that I like laughing better!"

Even at home Uncle Nachum was a tease, barking like a dog, mewing like a cat, and frightening Aunt Devorah time after time.

"You ought to be ashamed!" she would scold him. "The head of a family, the father of grown sons, making a fool of yourself like some delinquent! You old rascal! You're a disgrace to me! What's got into you?"

It was obvious from the way she spoke that Aunt Devorah wasn't angry with him. The trace of a smile flickered at the corners of her mouth. I suspected that Aunt Devorah was amused by her husband's pranks but did not want to admit it.

Perhaps my aunt was right. There was some evil spirit in Uncle Nachum, causing him to fool people. When he had the urge, there was no power in the world that could stop him. He played his tricks in muffled joy, quietly. During the act he was as tense as a juggler, whose success depends on every turn of his hand.

My uncle played many pranks. To tell about them all, I'd have to write a whole book. So I'll have to be satisfied with only one story, the story of Uncle Nachum's greatest prank. I saw it with my own eyes.

One day I noticed that Uncle Nachum had changed. That bright face of his and those eyes flashing in mischief were gone. I didn't have to ask what had caused his dark mood. Uncle Nachum told me.

"This morning I was depressed. You know, of course, that I'm deep in debt. So what do I do? I borrow from one person to pay back the other. I borrow from a third to pay back the second. That way I manage to keep going. But now I owe my landlord so much back rent that he's threatening me with eviction. I had to go and ask Gedalyah to lend me some money for a little while. But he, the skinflint, just pointed at his stuffed dog and answered—no, you guess what he answered!"

I kept still. Uncle Nachum waited a minute before telling me, mimicking Uncle Gedalyah's voice.

"This dog will bark before you get a cent out of me!"

I'd never seen Uncle Nachum in such low spirits. It was no

wonder my heart ached. I was sorry about his trouble and at the same time incensed at my stingy Uncle Gedalyah. I wanted to say something to Uncle Nachum to cheer him up, but I was very young and I couldn't put it into words.

Before long I was to see Uncle Nachum's revenge.

The next week he came to me and said, "Come on, let's go and see Gedalyah."

"What?" I looked at him in amazement, remembering the disappointment that had been his fate in his brother's home. Uncle Nachum winked at me with a childlike sparkle in his eyes. I knew that look very well and guessed that an amusing adventure was in store for me.

We went to Uncle Gedalyah's home. His wife was out shopping. As he let us in, Uncle Gedalyah nodded a cold greeting and said with a whine, "I'm very busy! I'm in a meeting with lumber dealers. But since you're here, go on into the living room." Then he returned to his office and slammed the door.

Uncle Nachum hesitated a moment, like a tightrope walker about to take his first step. The next minute he went up to the stuffed dog, bent down, picked it up, and took it into the adjoining bedroom. Then he said to me, "I'm going out a minute. Wait for me at the door. I'll leave it open." And he ran down the stairs.

A moment later Uncle Nachum appeared on the stairs with Rex, Stefan the doorman's dog, on a leash. He went into the living room, walked over to the place where the stuffed dog had sprawled, removed the leash, and commanded Rex to sit. Rex sprawled there, completely still, a huge, gray German shepherd, its big teeth bared and its red tongue hanging out of its mouth.

Uncle Nachum took my hand and drew me over to the table. We both sat down, waiting for Uncle Gedalyah. At last he appeared in the living room, scowling and raising his bushy eyebrows.

"I don't like disturbances during my business hours!" he snapped angrily.

Uncle Nachum addressed him in a humble tone. "Gedalyah, these are hard times for me. Last week I told you about the rent I owe my landlord. He's about to serve notice of eviction. So I have to beseech you please to do me this kindness. I give you my word that I'll pay you back next week."

Now I understood why Uncle Nachum had asked me to accompany him. He must have hoped my presence would influence his brother not to refuse. But I saw my error soon enough. No, Uncle Nachum entertained no such illusions. He had planned a trick and wanted an audience.

Uncle Gedalyah hardened his heart. His face was flushed. He raised his fist, waving it at Rex, who sprawled where the stuffed dog had been, and he shouted, "I told you that dog will bark before you get a cent out of me!"

Rex saw the fist waving at him and leaped up, barking mightily and springing at Uncle Gedalyah.

Uncle Gedalyah turned pale as a ghost. He drew back, his eyes bulging. He gaped and wanted to scream, but the scream caught in his throat. He stood there a minute, his hands twitching as if he wanted to defend himself from the charging dog. All at once he swayed and would have fallen if Uncle Nachum hadn't rushed to his support and commanded Rex to sit.

Through all this I was seated at the table, my heart beating fast. It seemed to me that I too had turned pale. Wide-eyed, I looked on.

Uncle Gedalyah was stretched out on the sofa with his eyes closed. Uncle Nachum ran to the kitchen, brought a glass of water, and poured it on the fainting man's face. When Uncle Gedalyah opened his eyes and regained consciousness, Uncle Nachum turned to Rex, took the leash out of his pocket, and fastened it to the dog's collar. Then he directed a single word to me: "Out!"

So we took our leave of Uncle Gedalyah. Uncle Nachum strode out first, holding the leash, and I was behind him. Once we were downstairs, Uncle Nachum tied Rex to the gate again.

Uncle Nachum walked away slowly, his rigid hand gripping mine. I thought that as soon as we had moved away a little he would stop and burst into a tremendous laugh, louder than I'd ever heard. Why, just now I'd seen him play his greatest prank.

But Uncle Nachum walked on in silence. For a minute it even seemed he was sighing. I looked up and gazed at his face. A tear rolled from his eye and dropped to his cheek. He didn't bother to wipe it off.

CONCERNING CATS, A PHOTOGRAPHER, AND GRANDMA LEAH

Uncle Nachum was a man of many pranks. Some are still etched in my memory, some forgotten. Pranks that came about casually, unthinkingly, and others that were planned carefully. They all had one thing in common: all of them taught me to see life's absurdities and laugh at them.

I liked to walk in the street with Uncle Nachum and see the spark of mischief suddenly flash in his eyes. I watched his facial expressions, astonished at their range. Uncle Nachum was a great mimic. As they passed him, the people in the street seemed to trigger his inner mechanism for mimicry. Now he'd straighten his head, thrust out his belly, and blow up his cheeks, and his face would take on the expression of the large, stout Jew striding our way at that moment. The next thing you knew, he'd be pinched in and small, frowning, all of him an astounding resemblance to that poor woman standing on the corner.

Those were little tricks, ones he just pulled out of his sleeve. He also had genuine escapades in store, ones he planned scrupulously, devoting much time and thought to them so as to achieve his object, which was to fool people and laugh.

I remember one of those great escapades in particular. It was on April Fools' Day. That morning I got up as usual, ready to go to school. But as I sat down at the table for breakfast, my sister Sarenka's voice reached my ears, a flustered, excited voice.

"Did you see it, Benny?"

"What?"

"The ad."

"What ad?"

Sarenka handed me the newspaper. On the last page, in a handsome frame, this advertisement was printed:

> WE BUY CATS, ONE GOLD PIECE PER CAT.
> THE CATS ARE TO BE DELIVERED EARLY IN THE MORNING.

Lower down, in small type, the address appeared:

Market Lane, Praga.

Praga, a suburb of Warsaw, lay on the other side of the river that divided the city, quite a distance from our neighborhood. The distance did not deter my sister, however.

"We'll make plenty of money," said Sarenka. "There's no shortage of cats in the yard. We'll each catch one and take them to Praga."

"What about school?" I asked.

"You don't get a chance like this every day!" my sister replied. "Let's get busy. If we're quick, maybe we'll make it to the second class."

I didn't need persuasion. To my mind, a gold piece was real money, the kind I rarely acquired. I filled a bowl with milk and went down to the yard. Before I had a chance to set it on the ground under the chestnut tree, a bunch of little cats magically appeared from the back yard and pounced on the milk. Sarenka and I, having emptied our briefcases previously, each grabbed a kitten by the back of the neck, dropped them into the briefcases, fastened the buckles, and were off. The kittens wailed at first, but soon they were quiet.

We left the Jewish quarter hurriedly and set out for the river. Approaching the bridge, we began to notice large parties of children and adults plodding in the same direction. Some walked with woven baskets in their hands, some with wooden boxes, and some, like us, clutched briefcases. Most of the children held their cats in their arms. It was a grand cat show: black ones and white ones, yellow and brown and striped. From all the streets and alleys groups of people streamed, like little brooks flowing into a great river. We made slow progress, packed in the mighty throng of humans and cats. We were all headed for Praga, the suburb on the other side of the bridge.

As I was walking, I looked up and suddenly stopped. In the boulevard, on a bench near the bridge, I noticed my Uncle Nachum. He was sitting there at his ease, puffing on a cigar. His laughing eyes followed the march of children and adults. I nudged Sarenka with my elbow and pointed at my uncle. My sister cast me an indifferent glance and went on walking.

"So what?" she said. "Everyone's going! Are you afraid of Uncle?"

Sarenka didn't catch on. I had to grab her hand and pull her over to the bench where Uncle Nachum was sitting.

At first he didn't notice us, since his laughing eyes never left the vivid parade. But if I'd had any doubts, now at the sight of the sparks dancing in his eyes I knew I was right.

"Good morning, Uncle Nachum," I said.

Our uncle turned to look at us and feigned surprise. "What are you doing here at this hour?" he asked innocently.

I kept still. I looked at his eyes. Sarenka tried to hide behind my back.

Uncle Nachum pretended he was scolding us. "Why haven't you gone to school?" he asked.

Instead of answering I sat down beside him, took my briefcase off my back, and unfastened the buckles. The kitten sprang out and ran and hid behind a tree trunk.

"What are you doing?" Sarenka rebuked me. "You've just thrown away a gold piece!"

Hearing this, Uncle Nachum burst into a mighty laugh. I let my voice join his, and Sarenka looked at us with gaping eyes. She must have believed we'd lost our senses.

When we'd calmed down a little, I asked, "April Fools' Day?" Uncle Nachum nodded.

"And it was you who put the ad in the paper?"

"Who else?" asked Uncle Nachum in reply, and once again he burst into thundering laughter. Then all at once his laugh stopped short, and his face took on a look of alarm. While we wondered about this change in his mood, we saw his wife, Aunt Devorah, striding to the bridge in the midst of the streaming crowd, a big, spotted cat in her arms.

At the sight of his wife, Uncle Nachum darted from the bench. Before he began running for his life, he managed to throw us a word of warning.

"Don't you dare tell Auntie about my part in this parade!" Then he vanished.

Sarenka let her cat go, too. It was quite a job for us to squeeze into the crowd, swimming against the current, and work our way back to school.

That was a great prank for Uncle Nachum. He loved to fool people and certainly must have been satisfied this time. I admired his ingenuity and wanted to copy him very much. Of course, I couldn't come close to him. A prank on the order of the cat scheme was beyond my capacity. As the days went on and I spent more and more time in Uncle Nachum's company, I sensed that a little of his temperament had come off on me, and the sights I saw provided me, too, with ample material for jokes. Absurdities amused me. I laughed a lot, and my laugh, that of a child, was a sort of faint echo of the great, thundering laughter of Uncle Nachum.

I began to imitate the behavior of people. Avidly I observed the few guests who happened to call on our household. After they were gone I would make faces, mimicking their movements and manner of speaking. I was riveted to the windowpane, my eyes surveying the passers-by in the yard; they too served as my models. My sister Sarenka was my "audience." It was for her I put on my shows, interrupted only by our side-splitting laughter.

At first, Father didn't understand what was going on. He was too busy with his affairs. Then one day he came into the room and caught me in the act. I had been showing how Antony the doorman walked as he popped out of his cellar apartment, half-drunk, clenching his hand to hold up his pants, which had come loose at the seams and which he was afraid of losing. Sarenka followed me with flashing eyes, and my mouth was full of gleeful laughter.

Father fixed his sad eyes on me, raised his eyebrows, and promptly scolded me. "What's so funny? And what's a Jewish boy doing laughing, anyway? Do you think you're some foolish gentile, getting drunk and laughing like a wild man? You just wait. You'll be crying before the day is out!"

He knew what he was talking about. For in the long run, tears came more frequently to us children than laughter. That very day I was beaten up by Stashek, Antony's assistant. Our home truly was not the proper place for frivolity and laughter. Whenever I wanted to unloose my urge for practical jokes, I fled the house and its worrisome gloom. I ran to my favorite childhood haunt, the public park.

The park was like an oasis to us in our desert of walls. In the morning young mothers rested on its benches, smiling at their babies. Older women knitted industriously. Idle old men sat by the lake, chatting. In the afternoon, when school was out, the park was full of bands of vociferous children playing cops and robbers, tag, or football. The noisy city beyond the fence seemed to recede and vanish. We were enclosed on all sides by plane trees, with their heavy boughs, acacias, whose tops arched above us, and soaring poplars and pines, their greenery glistening. Lilac bushes thrust bunches of purple flowers before our eyes, and we luxuriated in their fragrance.

There were plenty of lovely places in the park. At its far end was the greenhouse, with its walls of sparkling glass. Within it, wondrous tropical trees bloomed, and a tiny pool held flitting fish that left a wake of gold in their path. In the very center of the park was a pile of stones covered with green moss; from a hidden crack at the top, a jet of water poured, descending in a cascade and splashing down to the bottom. The water rushed and bubbled. I would stand there, by the cascade, and think to myself, *That's the rock that Moses struck!*

Opposite the cascade a hill rose high, with a slope on either side. We used to hold races from its peak, galloping down the hillside, borne on invisible wings. We used the hill for another game, too: we adopted it as our Mount Sinai. We used to stand at the bottom, lifting our eyes on high and pricking up our ears. We almost expected to see the thunder and the lightning. One day Shimek the redhead lit a bonfire on top of the hill, in fulfillment of the scripture, "And Mount Sinai was wrapped in smoke." But the park patrolman swiftly arrived and we, the Children of Israel, left our revelation on Mount Sinai and fled for our lives.

In the autumn the park afforded us another game. The chestnuts ripened and we picked them. Some of us used poles with nails or loops at their tips, while others hurled sticks that pierced the dark foliage at the treetop, jolting the chestnuts from their recesses and knocking them to the ground. The chestnuts weren't fit to eat, but we gathered them painstakingly, sackfuls of them!

I still haven't recounted all the wonders of the park.

At the entrance, in a niche between the walls, a street photographer took his post. This was Mr. Feldman, a tall Jew with a large, felt hat casting its shade on his bald head, a black mustache over-running the corners of his mouth and dangling to his chin, and eyes that peered through thick spectacles. Mr. Feldman had a big camera, a sort of square box perched on a tripod, with a "sleeve" hanging at the rear. Actually the "sleeve" was a curtain of black cloth into which the photographer would slip his head and hands as he worked. Facing the camera was a dummy airplane, painted on cloth. The children to be photographed would sit on the wooden seat in the dummy, gripping the painted control stick as their eyes sparkled with joy. In the picture they'd look like real pilots! Behind the camera, on a wooden bench, were bowls containing a dark liquid in which Mr. Feldman immersed the developed pictures.

We spent many hours in Mr. Feldman's corner, watching the children come with their mothers to have their pictures taken. We wanted very much to be photographed, but we were penniless. We never had our pictures taken, but we were interested in the process. We watched as a boy sat down in the dummy and Mr. Feldman pushed his felt hat back on his forehead, stared through his glasses, and plunged into the black "sleeve" that dropped to his shoulders, there to perform his wizardry in the dark.

Mr. Feldman never chased us away. He was a friendly, good-natured person. Only when we crowded too close to the camera would he reprove us with a smile, saying, "Go away, you little devils!"

So the park was an enchanting, captivating playground for us. The sounds of our laughter rose in its midst. All our heart's desires that were suppressed at home had their fling there, unrestrained.

But one day I cried in the park. This is how it happened.

Uncle Nachum's mother lived with him at home, an old, thin, shriveled woman whose eyes were dull with age. Everyone called her Grandma Leah. Uncle Nachum performed his filial duty to her, taking care of all her needs, strolling with her every evening in the park, and hurrying to fulfill her every wish. Of course, his instinct got the better of him at times, and then he would not refrain from playing tricks on his mother. One day he burst into the house, panting and sweating, and loudly announced, "Mother, you won a lottery!"

Grandma Leah raised her dim eyes to her son. "How could it be?" she wondered. "I didn't buy a ticket!"

"Who needs a ticket?" replied Uncle Nachum. "If you're lucky, you win a lottery even without a ticket!"

I was astonished at Uncle Nachum, fooling his mother that way, but at the sight of the mischievous spark in his eye I understood that he'd been powerless to resist the temptation.

Another time I dropped in on Uncle Nachum and heard him chatting with Aunt Devorah. My aunt said, "Grandma Leah's going to be eighty next week, and we don't have a single photograph of her."

"I'm afraid to have her picture taken." Uncle Nachum tried to joke, as usual. "They'll see her picture in Hollywood and abduct her. All in the pursuit of beauty."

At once he became serious. It seemed as if he bit his tongue. "You're right, Devorah," he said thoughtfully. "We should have a photograph of her to keep."

Then and there it was decided. Next week, God willing, they would go to Mr. Feldman and have Grandma Leah's picture taken.

The next day, when I came to see Uncle Nachum, Grandma Leah was at home alone. As I came in, I noticed that a cloud of worry had settled on Grandma Leah's face. She sat in an armchair, her tiny form bunched up. She was silent for a moment. Then suddenly she lifted her dim eyes to me and asked, "Does it hurt, Benny?"

I didn't catch the meaning of her question. "What, Grandma Leah?"

"Well, the picture . . ." the old woman stammered. "You know, I never had my picture taken, and now I'm scared a little."

Just then I saw Uncle Nachum in my mind's eye, and I was

sorry he couldn't hear this conversation. How would Uncle Nachum have answered Grandma? All at once I felt a sting in my eyes. I knew that if I'd looked in a mirror I would have seen that familiar spark of mischief. How had the spark flown from Uncle Nachum's eyes straight into mine?

Unable to hold my tongue, I heard myself say, "Don't worry, Grandma. It's like having a tooth pulled. Just ask Mr. Feldman to give you an injection first. Then it won't hurt."

Grandma Leah smiled a toothless smile. She must have been relieved.

At last the great day arrived. Uncle Nachum, Aunt Devorah, their son Eli, and I set out for Mr. Feldman's place in the park. Grandma Leah walked in our midst, mincing along. The passersby turned and looked back at us. They seemed astonished at the appearance of Grandma Leah, her shoulders wrapped in a black holiday shawl and a white kerchief, studded with pearls, on her head. Uncle Nachum blew smoke rings from his cigarette. Eli, a big fellow, looked at me crossly and muttered, "Who asked you to come along!"

Uncle Nachum silenced him. "Leave the boy alone. What do you want from him?"

At last we reached our destination. At the sight of our party, Mr. Feldman removed his felt hat, stroked his long mustache, and bowed. "Please sit down."

I wondered if Grandma Leah actually was going to sit in the dummy airplane and hold the control stick. That would have made a funny picture, Grandma the pilot!

Mr. Feldman seated Grandma in a straw chair. She sat there, small and wrinkled, her face rather pale. Mr. Feldman promptly went over to his camera and began fixing the "sleeve" behind it, while we, the family, stood aside, holding our breath.

Just then Grandma Leah's faint voice was heard. "Mr. Feldman!"

The photographer dropped his black cloth and went over to Grandma. "What is it, madame?" he asked.

Grandma Leah lifted her pale face to him and stammered, "Maybe, sir, you could give me an injection first?"

Mr. Feldman froze in bewilderment.

At this point, Eli jumped as if a snake had bitten him and yelled, "What are you babbling about, Grandma? What injection?"

"So it won't hurt," said Grandma Leah softly, babyishly.

"Who put that nonsense into your head?" Eli screamed.

Grandma Leah raised her little hand, and her bony finger pointed at me. I blushed. *I'd better get out of here fast,* I thought. But Eli's hand was quicker than my thought. He waved it mightily and slapped me on both sides, two ringing smacks that brought stars to my eyes.

"Take that and remember not to play jokes on Grandma!" he yelled at me. "You're a disgrace to us. I'm going to teach you a lesson!"

Eli apparently regarded those slaps as merely a down payment. From the look on his face, it was clear he meant to tear me to shreds. Just then Uncle Nachum intervened. At first, when Grandma Leah requested the injection, Uncle Nachum was struck dumb. Once he grasped the plain truth of the matter, however, that familiar spark of mischief appeared in his eyes. Now he hurried over, raising his hand to shield me from his son's fury, and scolded him.

"Don't you dare hit the boy! Do you hear?"

Then he gave me an affectionate, playful smile and whispered, "Well, you're a chip off the old block. Don't cry, Benny. Eli's a hothead. He's too stupid to understand a joke!"

But I fled, running straight down the park paths and crying loudly. And the trees about me, plane trees and acacias, poplars and pines, seemed to be nodding their heads sympathetically, as though they felt for me in my humiliation.

THE PEST

There were thirty children in our class, all of us imprisoned between the school walls while we longed to be outside playing. All of us afraid of the teacher's voice, which might call us to the blackboard. All of us in dread of tests.

But in spite of all we had in common, we were not alike. In our class were the four sons of the Passover Haggadah, the wise one, the wicked one, the simple one, and the one who could not ask a question. And there were others too—a decent one and a cheat; a fighter for justice, who cast caution to the winds in his struggle against unfairness; and an apathetic one, who cared for himself alone. There was a brawny one and a puny one, a clown and an eternally earnest type—each child with a look and character of his own.

Goldin was quite different in appearance from the other children of the class. His red hair shone; even his freckled face glowed like a flame. His father, a prosperous merchant, had a jewelry store on one of the main streets of the city. In this regard as well, Goldin was an exception among the children of the class, whose fathers were mostly petty merchants or poor tradesmen.

Goldin always came to school dressed in fine clothes, his shoes shiny and his briefcase, of expensive leather, fitted with copper buckles. His pockets jingled with coins, since his father granted him a generous allowance. During recess, Goldin used to run out to the nearby refreshment stand and buy himself a slice of cake or a big scoop of ice cream. It never occurred to him to treat his friends.

We didn't envy him. Each of us had pleasures of his own. But Goldin used to get our goat. That was why we took to calling him "The Pest." Actually, we all detested Goldin, and he, on his part, did everything he could to earn our hatred.

During the longest recess, we used to empty our briefcases of the snacks our mothers had packed for us before we left for school. There was no great variety in the menu: bread and butter or jam, a sandwich of yellow cheese or herring. Food in hand, we would rush outside to play in the yard. Goldin was the only one who remained in class. He would spread a white napkin on the bench and take out soft rolls, different kinds of salami, meat, and fine, rare fruits. The sight of these delicacies would make our mouths water, but we pretended to take no notice of the delectable fare. Goldin nevertheless constantly tried to attract our attention. In the morning, upon arriving in class, he took out his rolls, waved them in front of our eyes, stuck out his big, red tongue, licked them, and loudly announced, "Look! I licked my food!" The implication was clear. Since I have, you won't be tempted to steal a taste of it!

Such a thing never occurred to us. We hated Goldin and extended our hatred to his provisions as well. Let him eat his fill and choke on it! His teasing disgusted us. More than once we had the urge to let him have what he deserved, but in the end we acted as if he never existed.

Among the children in the class was a fighter for justice, who was always ready to risk everything in his struggle against unfairness. His name was Berman. One day, before the first lesson, Goldin was summoned to the office for some reason or other, and then Berman moved into action. He took Goldin's rolls out of his briefcase, dipped them in the toilet bowl, and hung them up on a string tied to the blackboard. I, being good at rhymes, wrote on the blackboard:

Look and think well, you thieving soul:
This food has been dipped in the toilet bowl.
True, it was licked by no tongue of mine,
But I dare anyone else to dine!

I signed it, "The Pest."

Goldin came back, and when he glanced at the blackboard his flushed face grew crimson. He rushed out and returned with the principal. The principal stood there a minute looking at the blackboard and at us, and then he quietly asked, "Who did it?"

The class was silent. We could have heard a fly beating against the windowpane.

"Who did it?" the principal asked again.

Berman got up and said, "I'm the one who dipped the rolls in the toilet."

"Why did you do that?"

"To teach him not to annoy us!"

"How does he annoy you?"

"With the fresh rolls he brings from home and all that food of his!"

"Are you jealous of him?"

"Not at all! But he really wants us to be jealous of him. Before eating, he licks his rolls to make us jealous of him so that we can't ask him for a taste."

"And that goes on every day?"

"Yes, every day, sir!"

I was afraid of the storm that was about to descend upon Berman, so I roused my courage and stood up.

"I wrote the rhyme," I said.

The principal stood there a minute, taking a long look at Goldin. Then he turned without a word and left the class.

Goldin never learned his lesson. He was thick-skinned, and our powerful hatred could do nothing to hurt him. He was tall, but it was a wonder to me how he had the pluck to stand up all alone to his twenty-nine classmates. He never let us alone, annoying and plaguing us. He talked about the films he'd seen and the camps he'd gone to on his vacation. In the summer he was at the seaside; in the winter he was in the mountains, where he went skiing. We listened and kept still, ignoring him and his stories.

Goldin was particularly harassing to Rashkes, whose father was a poor cobbler. During vacations, Rashkes worked to help support his family. Rashkes wore patched pants and worn-out shoes. In the winter he used to come to school in his older brother's coat, which since it was much too big, he would fasten to his waist with a broad leather belt. I still remember the buckle of that belt, a big buckle, square and rusty. Every time Goldin came across Rashkes, he seized the opportunity for provocation. He began by saying, "Listen, Rashkes, the apartment above ours belongs to a doctor, but you have a shoemaker under your place."

"So what?" replied Rashkes, and not a muscle on his face moved. We would have liked to see him charge that swaggering Goldin and give him a beating. But Rashkes was short and only reached Goldin's shoulders.

Goldin kept rankling him. "Rashkes, the patch on your pants is coming off! You can see everything!"

"So what?" Rashkes would reply, quietly.

"Rashkes," Goldin taunted him, "where did you ever find that leather belt? You could kill someone with it! Did you steal it from a porter? Fellows," he turned to us, "I propose that from now on we call Rashkes 'The Porter'!"

Although Rashkes made no response, it was obvious that Goldin's words cut him to the quick. We were silent. Even Berman, the fighter for justice, didn't fight for little Rashkes's honor. Not because he was afraid of Goldin. As I said, we all despised him and ignored his presence. If the matter had occurred today, we would have some caustic epithets available, but then we made do with calling him "The Pest." Nevertheless, that nickname was capable of expressing the full force of our hatred.

One winter day two teachers were sick, and at recess time the principal sent us home. We rushed out cheering, like a herd galloping out of its pen. We were greeted by a bright sun whose rays were reflected in the snow, dazzling us. We took a deep breath of the chilly, clear air. We were intoxicated with freedom.

"Let's go down to the river and slide on the ice!" exclaimed Greenberg, the leader of the class.

The river was very wide. The city was built on either side of it, with a bridge across it. On our way to the river, as we passed Goldin's house, he left us for a minute and came back with a pair of ice skates with gleaming iron runners fastened to their soles. Finally we reached the riverside and threw our briefcases down in a great heap.

The water on both banks was frozen, a solid surface of ice covered by soft snow. It was only between them, in the middle, that the water remained unfrozen. There it flowed in a stream, its waves crowned with foam. Here and there chunks of ice were borne along in the current, swept downstream. These chunks piled up against the abutments of the bridge. We could hear the noise of the water and the chunks of ice grating as they scraped against one another.

We made a dash for the river and went sliding on it. At first we ran a little, but then we stopped all at once. As our shoes slid by the force of inertia and carried us, we imagined we'd grown wings and were fluttering in the air. The wind whistling in our ears, we let out cries of joy.

We were careful not to get too close to the middle of the river, fearing we wouldn't be able to stop and would fall into the crack, where the foaming water flowed. We were hot from running, so we took off our coats and put them down in the snow. Rashkes, who had no woolen clothing, remained in his oversized coat fastened with the broad leather belt.

As we slid one after the other, marking out a firm, mirror-smooth path in the soft snow that covered the ice, Goldin left us. Wearing his ice skates, he passed us like lightning and turned circles, spinning on one leg. The ice responded with a rasping hiss, and snowflakes leaped like sparks from the iron runners of his skates. When Goldin moved away from us we thought nothing of it, since we couldn't bear his company anyway. Then, all of a sudden, we heard a cry of terror, and the voice was Goldin's.

Goldin had skated to the edge of the crack. The ice, thin and brittle there, had broken, and Goldin found himself drifting on a chunk of ice that was swept along in the rushing current.

We forgot that the one who was waving his hands and screaming for help was the hated Goldin. Panic-stricken, as if stunned by thunder, we burst into a run, trying to keep up with the chunk of ice that floated in the current. We were afraid to approach the crack, since the ice might have broken under our weight. We shivered, our hair on end, as we ran along the ice, joining voices with Goldin and his cries of "Help!"

But there was no one else nearby. We were far from shore. We could see only Goldin's contorted face when he stooped and gripped the chunk of ice so as not to fall off. His crimson face was white as the surrounding snow.

Helplessly we ran after the chunk of ice. Just then we noticed that little Rashkes had overtaken us and turned toward the big crack. We still did not grasp what was happening.

"Watch out, Rashkes! The ice beneath you will break!" we yelled.

Rashkes never looked back. He moved closer to the crack and ran alongside it, even overtaking Goldin.

The chunk with Goldin on it floated in a winding path. Sometimes it approached the edge of the crack and then moved away, and sometimes it spun around like a drunkard. Then, suddenly, it drifted very close to where Rashkes stood.

"Put out your hand!" yelled Rashkes. Just then a great chunk of ice came up from behind and swept Goldin's chunk along with it.

Rashkes didn't give up. He dashed on alongside the crack. We ran after him, closer to shore, on the solid ice. All at once we caught our breath in terror. The ice broke beneath Rashkes, and one of his legs sank up to the knee in water.

"Come back, Rashkes, come back!" we screamed.

Rashkes took no notice of our cries. He withdrew his leg from the cold water and continued his pursuit of Goldin.

Again Goldin's chunk of ice approached the edge of the crack. Goldin and Rashkes reached out to each other, but the distance between them was too great. In the meantime the ice was borne along and drew close to an abutment of the bridge. If it hit the abutment, it would smash and Goldin would be lost!

Then we saw Rashkes stop and remove the broad leather belt from his waist. He held the big buckle and flung the end of the belt to Goldin.

"Catch!"

Goldin stuck out his hands and missed. Rashkes threw it again.

"Catch!"

This time Goldin managed to grasp the end of the belt.

Rashkes gripped the buckle and never let go. He was afraid that Goldin, who was bigger and heavier, would drag him into the water. So he stretched out alongside the crack, hugging the ice with his whole body. With his hand holding the buckle, he pulled and slowly drew Goldin and his chunk of ice close. We followed the scene with pounding hearts.

"A little bit more!"

"Almost!"

"Hurray! He saved him!"

The next morning Goldin was no better. He never apologized to Rashkes. He never thought to give him a word of thanks. But when the bell sounded, announcing that recess time had arrived, Goldin took two snack bags out of his briefcase. He kept one for himself and offered the other to Rashkes, saying, "Here, this is for you."

Little Rashkes looked up at Goldin, took the bag from him, went up to the wastebasket, and threw it in.

We finished our homework and went out, as usual, to play hide-and-seek in the nearby city park. It was a day like any other, the same sky overhead, the same treetops in the park, swaying in the breeze. But this day has remained in my mind, since it was about to change our daily routine.

All five of us were there: Sevek, Shimek, Kubah, Edek, and me. As we dashed about, searching for a thick tree trunk or a clump of bushes to hide behind, Sevek stopped by a flower bed and bent his head attentively. Surprised, we went up to him and lent an ear. From the thicket of stems and blossoms a high voice emerged, something between a cheep and a shriek.

The flower beds were fenced in, and it was forbidden to walk on them. The park watchman was stationed there, making his rounds every day, holding a long stick with a nail at its tip. The watchman would pierce the papers scattered on the lawn with his nail, picking them up and throwing them into the garbage pail. As he did this, he observed what was happening in the park, and woe to the child who was caught in a flower bed. The watchman's stick would whack the offender on his back and head.

Sevek stood by the flower bed and looked about. We caught on and spread out on the adjoining paths, our eyes scouring the park. The watchman had vanished. It seemed the earth had opened its mouth and swallowed him. We waved Sevek on. He jumped over the fence, rummaged through the flowers, and returned a minute later, carrying a little, whimpering puppy, its eyes closed.

"We have a dog!" announced Sevek.

We crowded close, each of us putting out his hand and stroking the puppy. We sensed its warmth, the quiver that shook its skin. Our hearts melted with pity for the tiny, helpless creature. From the very first we clung to it in love.

We children of the yard had never kept animals. No dog, no cat, no canary. The animals that dwelt in our midst were nothing but a source of trouble. They were the flies that bothered us during the day and the bedbugs that bit us at night. There were rats too, darting with shrill squeals among the stockrooms in the back yard and terrifying us. Now, all at once, we came by a real find, this darling puppy!

The puppy was black as pitch. Only its forehead glistened like a white star.

"What breed is it?" asked Shimek.

Sevek was at a loss. Even he, the leader of the group, was no expert at dogs and their breeds. "What difference does it make?" he said. "He's still small and it's hard to tell. All puppies look alike. After he grows a little, we'll be able to tell his breed."

Of course, we didn't go on playing hide-and-seek. We returned to our yard. Sevek strode ahead of us, holding the puppy in his arms.

"Where are we going to keep it?" asked Kubah. "We can't just take it home!"

Kubah was right. Our parents would be against the idea of a dog in the house. I knew there would be no use pleading with my father. "What do you mean?" Father would scold me. "Dogs are for gentiles, not Jewish boys!"

We sat underneath the chestnut tree and held a conference. It was Sevek who solved our problems. He took the puppy in his arms and went with it to the back yard. At the entrance to one of the stockrooms, there was a high, broad stoop made out of boards. Its sides were open at the bottom.

"Our doghouse will be here, under the steps," Sevek decided. "We'll close off one side with a board and we'll make a door on the other side."

Before long Edek brought some boards, and Shimek a hammer and nails. Sevek did the job. He closed up one side and on the other fastened a little door, which could only open outwards. Meanwhile Edek ran home and brought back a glass of milk and a metal bowl. Sevek poured the milk into the bowl and offered it to the puppy. It stuck out a little red tongue and lapped it up. Its whining stopped.

"He needs a name," I said.

Many names were suggested: Rex, Sambo, Ralph, Spunky, Blacky. Then Sevek said, "Look at him lapping up that milk! Let's call him Lappy!"

Lappy emptied the bowl. We put him in his kennel, which we had padded with a sack, and we placed a big stone at the door.

"And now," Sevek said, "let's decide how we're going to take care of him."

After a stormy debate we agreed to divide the chores. Sevek would train Lappy, teaching him to obey commands such as "Down!" "Up!" and "Catch!" Edek was in charge of feeding him. Shimek would bring the water. Kubah would see that the kennel was clean.

"What about me?" I asked. "Why did you leave me out?"

"Take it easy!" Sevek reassured me. "There'll be a job for you too."

As we sat on the steps talking, Lappy began whimpering again. At that moment Stashek appeared in the yard, moving toward us with an ear to the ground.

"Who's that whining there?" asked Stashek.

Stashek, a fellow of about twenty, was Antony the doorman's helper. They were the only gentiles living in our yard, which otherwise was occupied exclusively by Jews. Antony, an elderly Pole whose long, white mustache always bristled at the tips, spent most of his time in his cellar apartment next to the gate. He would sit on his couch, drinking his liquor or taking a snooze. At times he would raise a commotion by beating his wife, whose screams split the heart of heaven. All the work in the yard, such as cleaning the stairways and sweeping the court, was entrusted to Stashek, the former waif whom Antony, being childless, had taken in and reared and trained as his assistant. Stashek, a big, cunning young man, harassed us and plotted against us and never spared us a thrashing. It was no wonder we hated him and did our best to keep out of his way.

Now, when he appeared by the stockroom, we knew we were in trouble.

"Who's that whining there?" Stashek asked again.

We had no choice, so we shared our secret with him.

"We found a puppy," said Sevek. "We made a kennel for him here, under the stoop. We'll raise him, and when he's a big dog he'll guard the yard for you."

"Who wants your dog?" Stashek screamed. "He'll make the yard filthy and I'll have to clean it! No, there'll be no such thing! Give me the puppy. I'll drown him in the lake!"

Our hearts quivered. Would Stashek really carry out his threat?

"What's it to you, Stashek?" Shimek tried to soften his heart. "We'll do the cleaning. Lappy won't cause you any trouble."

But Stashek's heart was hard. "Give me the puppy right now!" he ordered.

"We'll make it up to you, Stashek. Just let us keep our puppy," said Sevek.

"You beggars, you don't have a cent to your name!" cried Stashek.

"We'll help you at your job," Sevek offered. "We'll sweep the yard, wash the stairs."

"No!" Stashek shouted. "That's all I need! What will Antony say when he sees you working instead of me?"

We thought that was the end. It seemed there was no way in the world to save Lappy. Then Stashek thought a minute and said, "All right, I'll let you keep the dog, but on one condition. You must work with me at night, packing cigarettes."

At this point an explanation is due.

In the country in which we lived, there were no private cigarette factories. The production was controlled by a monopoly, that is to say an exclusive license legally enforced by the government. The government manufactured the cigarettes and determined their price. Whoever violated this law was subject to a severe penalty. Stashek, with his meager salary, had found an additional source of income. He would buy tobacco on the black market, and during the night, while Antony drowsed by the locked front gate —getting up to open it when the bell rang and letting the night owls in—Stashek would begin his work. We looked on more than once.

Stashek had a little iron tube that opened lengthwise into two halves, with a wooden handle at its tip and a small rod. Stashek would open up the tube, fill it with tobacco, and close it again. Then he would slip it into a cylinder of thin paper and push the little rod in. The rod forced the tobacco out of the tube and into the paper. At every push, a single cigarette stuffed with tobacco dropped from the tube. Stashek would sell the cigarettes for less than the market price.

Now, as Stashek proposed that we assist him, we breathed in relief. Surely packing cigarettes was an easier task than cleaning the yard! More than once, watching Stashek bent over making his cigarettes, we wanted to try and do the same. But we never dared ask him. And now the fellow had come and offered to let us take part in his enterprise!

"We agree!" we cried in unison. "We'll help you, and you'll forget about the dog and let us keep it!"

Then and there we decided that we all would take turns helping Stashek. True, the job had to be done at night, away from spying eyes, but somehow we would find a way to slip out of the house.

And so it was. Night after night we took turns sneaking out to sit there with Stashek, who had acquired another device for packing cigarettes. At first the work amused us, filling the tube with tobacco, pushing the little rod, and watching the rounded cigarettes drop on the table. But Stashek oppressed us with a reign of hard labor. He periodically raised our quota. At first it was 100 cigarettes a night, then 150. In the end he expected us to keep to a quota of 200 cigarettes a shift!

Such a shift went on for hours. At times my eyes closed and my head sank down, but then Stashek would reward me with a slap and yell, "Get to work!" Tears filled my eyes, but I lovingly accepted it all. I knew that Lappy's life depended on me and my labors.

Finishing the job, I went back home to bed. There wasn't much time left to sleep. In the morning, getting up, I was tired and had dark circles under my eyes. Mother felt my forehead: "Maybe you're sick?" There were times when I fell asleep during a lesson at school. The teacher reprimanded me, my classmates laughed at me. But I lovingly accepted it all.

What were night work, fatigue, and disgrace to me? The main thing was that Lappy would not be taken away. Sure enough, the puppy repaid us for all that we suffered on his account.

Lappy grew. He ran after us in the yard, rubbing up against our legs, licking our hands. We no longer went to the park to play.

Our afternoons were devoted entirely to Lappy. Those were good times, the best of our days.

Like any other dog, Lappy responded with love and faithfulness to those who were good to him. He had only one fault: he never barked. It was as if his heart, that of a foundling, perceived that his presence in the yard was undesirable. Of course it was endured somehow, but he never could direct any excessive attention to himself. So he kept still, as if he were dumb.

Lappy was never a cause for dispute among us. From the time we adopted him, we rigorously adhered to our division of duties. Sevek trained him and taught him to obey commands such as "Down!" "Up!" "Run!" and "Catch!" Edek took care of his food, Shimek his water, and Kubah cleaned his kennel. Even I, after having been overlooked, finally won a job of my own.

One day Sevek said to me, "You, Benny, will teach Lappy to bark."

"How?" I asked.

"It's simple enough. Get down on all fours and bark. Lappy will listen and learn!"

I did it, but it turned out that either I was a poor teacher or Lappy was a negligent pupil. There was no use in my racing around before him on all fours, no use in my charging him, baring my teeth and emitting deafening barks. Lappy looked at me with his kind eyes and never uttered a sound. He kept still, as if he were dumb.

Summer passed and autumn arrived. One night I woke up to the sound of lightning, which shook the house. It was pouring outside. I lay awake a little while and all at once I remembered Lappy. The poor thing must be sprawling in his kennel, shivering with cold and fear!

I got stealthily out of bed, wrapped my head in a coat, and slipped outside to the back yard. I removed the stone by the kennel door and swept Lappy up in my embrace. And in truth, he was shivering greatly, his whole body shuddering. I went back home and lay in bed, hugging Lappy and clinging to him. His warmth flowed through my body. His tongue licked my face.

Fortunately, I awoke before dawn and managed to put the dog back in his kennel. At school, I never heard what the teacher said. The memory of that night was alive in me and warmed my heart.

Oh, how I loved Lappy!

Stashek demanded that we increase our quota, but our efforts were in vain. We couldn't manage to make more than 200 cigarettes a night. The night hours crawled by slowly. We sat there each in his turn, our hands doing the job as we fought off sleep.

We were slaves.

More than once as I sat opposite Stashek, packing the cigarettes with tobacco as my fingers grew limp with fatigue, I thought to myself, *It's true. I'm a slave.* But I accepted the yoke of slavery willingly, out of my love for Lappy. Didn't our forefather Jacob serve Laban the Aramean for fourteen whole years out of his love for Rachel?

Our trials were not yet over. One day Stashek informed us, "No more tobacco! From now on you have to bring it in by yourselves."

"What?" we said in amazement. "Where are we going to get tobacco?"

Stashek berated us and seethed, "You good-for-nothings! You each help me for only one night a week. It's time you applied yourselves to a real job! The streets are full of cigarette butts. There are plenty of high-class smokers who never finish more than half a cigarette. You pick up the butts, throw away the ashes, and keep the tobacco that's left."

We were silent. We had no choice.

From that day on we walked through the city streets, searching for cigarette butts. Having collected a pocketful, we went back to the yard, where beneath the chestnut tree we got down to work. We cut off the tips of cigarette ash with a scissors, unfastened the thin paper, and emptied the tobacco into a large box. When we were finished, Stashek came. He picked up the box as if estimating its weight, and that cunning grin of his never left his face.

The Passover holiday drew near. In school we studied the story of the Exodus from Egypt.

One day Sevek said to us, "Fellows, have you noticed that the same thing that happened to our forefathers in Egypt has happened to us? 'We were slaves of Pharaoh in Egypt'—and now we're the slaves of Stashek. At first he gave us 'mortar and bricks,' in other words tobacco to pack the cigarettes, and later we lived out the verses, "You shall no longer give the people straw to make bricks, as heretofore. Let them go and gather straw for themselves'! We too have been forced to go and gather tobacco. How long are we going to let that louse Stashek torture us?"

He was still speaking when Stashek's voice was heard from a corner of the yard. He must have been standing there, listening to our conversation.

"What did you say?" screamed Stashek. "Louse? I'll show you who's a louse!"

And he went up and punched Sevek in the jaw. Sevek bent his head and spit blood. A trickle of blood rolled down his chin.

We sprang up. If we had all charged Stashek together, he surely would have taken a beating. But we were children, Jewish children facing a gentile, and we couldn't muster up the courage to stand up to the bully and take revenge on him for Sevek. So we spread out, running through the yard and screaming with all our might, "Stashek is a louse! Stashek is a louse!"

Antony the doorman appeared in the doorway of his apartment. "What's going on?" he asked, gawking at us with drunken eyes.

We were dashing about the yard and shouting in unison, our voices rising in a mighty echo among the walls of the buildings, "Stashek is a louse!"

Stashek tried to catch us, but we were too quick and slipped out of his arms. In the end Stashek stopped, panting, waving his fist and crying at us furiously, "You just wait! I won't keep quiet about this!"

We rebelled.

The next day we didn't go out through the streets to collect cigarette butts. Stashek waited in vain for his daily box of tobacco. We didn't work at night any more, either. For a few days we tried avoiding Stashek, giving him a wide berth. Stashek kept still. Only his eyes peered at us viciously, ominously.

A week later, returning from school, we were struck by the commotion in the street. A large, barred wagon rolled by with dogs imprisoned in it, whining and barking loudly. Alongside the wagon strolled the dog catcher, a civil servant, and he held a long pole with a noose at its tip. He used this pole as a lasso to catch the ownerless dogs and lock them up in the wagon.

We were still looking on when Stashek appeared at our front gate with our Lappy in his arms.

Our hearts froze in terror. Before we could make a sound, Stashek went up to the dog catcher and winked at him. The dog catcher waved his pole and the noose tightened about our pet's neck. Lappy was hurled into the wagon. He stood there, by the bars, looking at us with his kind eyes, pleading for help.

Just then the wagon moved and Lappy opened his mouth in a tremendous bark, a strangled, heart-rending bark—the first of his life.

"My labors were not in vain," I thought. "At last Lappy's learned how to bark! But this first bark of his apparently is going to be his last. Surely all those dogs are doomed."

We dashed after the wagon. We waved our arms. We screamed. We cried. We pleaded. "Sir, let us have Lappy back, he's our dog."

Sevek clutched the rear end of the wagon and would not let go.

But the dog catcher threatened us with his pole, and we retreated. In a moment the wagon was gone.

Gloomily, mournfully, we went back home. Stashek stood at the gate, his hands in his pockets, whistling a merry tune to himself. As he noticed us, a smile spread on his face, a smile of spite. His cunning eyes regarded us tauntingly, malevolently, and then he opened his mouth.

"I kept my promise," he said. "Now you know who the louse is!"

We wanted to tear him apart, but we were small and helpless, Jewish children facing an evil gentile.

So it was that we were bereft of our beloved Lappy. We mourned for him and dreamed of vengeance, though we knew we were powerless to pay Stashek back.

Eventually we had our revenge.

Before many days had passed, the whole yard was in an uproar. Policemen, a sergeant at their head, appeared all at once in Antony the doorman's cellar apartment and searched it. That meant that somebody had informed them about Stashek. Before long the policemen discovered the devices for making cigarettes and several boxfuls of tobacco as well.

We ran out to the yard and peered at the scene in Antony's apartment. Stashek stood there, leaning on the wall, his face white as a sheet. Just then the sergeant turned to him and said, "So, you took it into your head to compete with the government and its tobacco monopoly, did you? Now you're going to prison and you'll have plenty of time to think about what you've done."

All at once Stashek broke away from the wall and sprang toward the door, but two policemen caught him between them. The sergeant punched him in the jaw. Stashek bent his head and spit blood.

We watched the policemen lead Stashek off with his hands in chains. A trickle of blood rolled down Stashek's chin. We wanted to cheer, but we were afraid of provoking the bully. After all, one day he would return from prison!

We stood in silence. Our eyes followed Stashek as he was swallowed up in the barred patrol wagon.

SEVEK'S FIRST SCENARIO

The movie house was located at the far end of the Jewish quarter, its entrance facing a Christian neighborhood, so that it was a kind of bridge connecting the two parts of the city. It was the only theater that screened matinees, and its audience was mostly children. Its facade sported enormous posters: Winatoo, the Apache chief, waving a lasso over his head; a sheriff out of the Old West shooting his two pistols from the hip; Tarzan pouncing on a leopard and holding it fast in a full nelson. The movies were changed twice a week. From three o'clock on, a long line of Jewish and Christian children extended from the box office, and the plaza in front of the movie house thronged with a noisy crowd. At exactly four o'clock the double doors opened wide. The excited, tumultuous crowd was engulfed within, and the bustling street emptied and was still.

We children of the yard would visit the movie-house plaza frequently, marveling at the vivid posters. We longed to go in and feast our eyes on the display of wonders we had learned of only by hearsay, but there was not a chance of our gaining entrance. The price of a ticket, forty cents, was beyond our means. One day Sevek took the plunge and tried to sneak in along with the flood of children going to see the show, but the usher noticed him, slapped him heartily, and kicked him out.

We went back to our yard with Sevek, whose cheeks were flaming. We sat down beneath the chestnut tree, gloomy and still. Shimek spoke first.

"Fellows, I've got an idea." Without waiting for encouragement, he disclosed his plan to us.

"Look, a ticket costs forty cents and there are five of us. I suggest that four of us get hold of ten cents each. We'll buy a ticket for the fifth boy and he'll go to the show."

"What will the generous contributors get out of it?" argued Kubah.

Shimek answered, "The lucky winner will tell us the plot of the movie, and in that way he'll pay for his ticket."

"And who is that lucky winner going to be?" I asked.

"We'll draw lots!" Shimek suggested.

"We'll take turns going to the shows!" contended Kubah.

Edek, who was Sevek's foremost ally, proclaimed, "I suggest we skip the lots and turns. Sevek is the oldest of us, and there's no doubt he knows best how to describe the plot of a movie. After all, he's always been interested in films."

At first it seemed as if Edek's proposal was unfair to us, but after consideration we had to admit that there was sense in what he said. Sevek really was a good storyteller. The allusion to his connection with the movies was not without foundation, either. Every time our conversation turned to the profession we would eventually choose, Shimek was of a firm mind. When he grew up he would be a coachman and drive around all day in a carriage! Kubah was determined to be an ice-cream vendor. Could anything be more delightful? You walk through the streets, a keg of ice cream on your back, and whenever you feel the urge you open it and gobble up as much as you want! Edek aspired to be a fireman. He would ride a white horse in front of the fire truck, his head gleaming with a copper helmet! I, who spent much of my time reading, dreamed of writing stories of adventure and travel. Sevek had always said, "When I grow up, I'm going to be a motion-picture director!"

So it turned out that Sevek came into a real prize. Then and there, it was decided to appoint him our loyal ambassador to the movie house. From then on we counted our pennies, each of us chipping in twenty cents a week. Every week Sevek went to two movies, on Tuesdays and Fridays. When the movie was over, we eagerly awaited him under the chestnut tree.

To tell the truth, Sevek never betrayed our hopes and trust. He described the movies he saw with the utmost fidelity, not omitting a single detail. There were times, in tense moments, when he raised his voice. And it happened that in his enthusiasm he actually began acting, playing the parts of the movie with real talent. We listened open-mouthed and said a silent prayer that the story would go on and on and never stop!

Sevek was gifted with a rich vocabulary and a considerable faculty for description. Hearing his stories, we actually could see the Apaches and the Sioux racing their wild horses across the prairies, and Winatoo, the noble chieftain, burying his tomahawk and making peace with his enemies. Once we went along with Captain Grant's children on their voyages, and another time we trailed the Headless Horseman. The sheriffs of the Wild West were old friends of ours. We knew every single one of them!

So it was that even if we'd been irritated at first by a sense of injustice and thoughts of drawing lots and taking turns, all was forgotten in the long run. Sevek gave each of us generous compensation for the twenty cents he received. Our meetings under the chestnut tree on Tuesday and Friday evenings put joy in our hearts.

Our spirits soon were darkened by an unceasing concern. Would we be able to fulfill our obligation? For the amassing of twenty cents involved tremendous difficulties.

We were poor children. True, we weren't starving. There was always a slice of bread to be had at home, and sometimes it was even buttered. Our fathers had a hard time supporting their households. Meat was on our menu on Sabbath days only. Once in a long while, on holidays, we were allowed to enjoy something new to wear. No luxuries spoiled us. The movies and summer camps were in dreamland, as far as we were concerned.

How, in spite of everything, did we get hold of twenty cents? Shimek rummaged around for old newspapers and supplied them for a few cents to a store that sold trinkets. Kubah picked up used bottles and sold them to a liquor store. Edek ran errands for shopkeepers. I sold an old book every once in a while. We each became experts in our fields. Yet at times in spite of all our efforts we still couldn't scrape the required twenty cents together, and so when everything else failed we pocketed some of the change we received when our mothers sent us to the grocery.

We were poor, but even poverty has ranks of its own. Sevek and his family were at the very bottom of the ladder. His father, a disabled veteran, used to sit at the gate of our house with his wooden leg stretched out before him, leaning on a small stand that displayed cigarettes, which he sold by the pack and singly. His face was always pale, and his eyes were sad. We knew what it cost him to get his bread.

There was plenty of snow that winter. Since Sevek's father sat outdoors all day, he caught a cold and was confined to his bed. When the cold developed into pneumonia, his condition became serious.

One Tuesday we sat under the chestnut tree and Sevek recounted the plot of a movie he had seen. As usual for him, he spoke at length of the sheriff and his war against the gangsters, and we followed the narrative breathlessly. Now the sheriff straightened up in his saddle, grabbed his rifle, and aimed it while galloping toward the bandit who was lurking for him behind the cliff. Sevek, in telling this, straightened where he sat and aimed, so to speak, the rifle in his hands.

All at once Shimek interrupted. "What do you mean? You told

us a minute ago that the sheriff was mortally wounded in the head, and the cowboys took him to the ranch!"

Sevek, momentarily embarrassed, became silent. He quickly recovered and snapped, "You dope! Pay attention and you won't get mixed up! I said it was the sheriff's deputy who was wounded, not the sheriff!"

He went on with the story, but we all knew that Shimek was right. It was Sevek who had gotten mixed up. Moreover, as Sevek went on spinning his tale, it became clear to us that we already had heard about the sheriff and the bandits. Why, a month ago Sevek had told us the very same story!

Three days passed. On Friday afternoon Shimek informed us, "Tonight we won't get together with Sevek!"

"What happened?" we said in astonishment. "We gave him forty cents!"

Shimek told us, "At five o'clock I happened to glance from my window and I saw Sevek coming out of the drugstore. Now the movie lasts from four until six!"

"Maybe Sevek had to stay with his father," Edek ventured. "He must have gone to get some medicine."

Downhearted, we decided to forgo the pleasure of Sevek's story. But toward evening Sevek appeared in the yard and summoned us with a whistle. At once we were all there by the chestnut tree—Shimek and Kubah, Edek and I. We waited to hear what he had to say.

"Fellows," said Sevek, "sit down and I'll tell you about the movie I saw today, *The Treasure of Silver Lake*, by Karl May."

"You liar!" Shimek exploded, always having been Sevek's rival and chief contender for the leader's crown. "You never even went to the movies! I saw you with my own eyes leaving the drugstore at five o'clock!"

Sevek's face grew red as a beet. He stood there a minute, his arms stretched out before him in a gesture of helplessness, but at once he shook it off and scolded Shimek.

"Shut up! You saw somebody else and thought it was me." Without giving us time for further reflection, Sevek began the story of *The Treasure of Silver Lake*.

All of us had read the book and were familiar with the plot. Sevek was faithful to the plot, but from the way he told it one could see that he was recounting the text and not the visions of the motion picture.

We were silent. We knew that Shimek was right. Sevek hadn't seen the movie. He was deceiving us. But we didn't dare make a sound. We were powerless to rebel against the authority that Sevek had imposed upon us for years.

Sevek kept it short this time. In a quarter of an hour he concluded his story and immediately got up and hurried home. We remained sitting under the chestnut tree, silent and avoiding each other's eyes.

Finally Shimek said bitterly, "The dirty liar! The filthy crook! I've been suspicious of him for a long time. Now it's clear beyond a doubt. Sevek hasn't been going to the movies at all. He's stealing our money. We won't let him get away with it!"

"Let him give us back the money!" cried Kubah.

"Who would have thought he would do such a thing?" mumbled Edek.

And Shimek repeated his pronouncement loudly. "Sevek is a crook! Sevek is a crook!"

As we took counsel to decide how we could get back at Sevek, we suddenly heard a sharp wail. We turned around. In the dark, in a corner of the yard, we saw Estusha, Sevek's little sister. She came up to our chestnut tree and stood among us, sobbing loudly.

I jumped up and took her by the shoulders. They were trembling. "Why are you crying, Estusha?" I asked.

"Sevek isn't a crook!" Estusha cried and covered her face in her hands.

When she had calmed down a little, she said, "Sevek never

cheated you. He always used to tell you about the movie! But for the past two weeks he hasn't been to the movies. Mother's been going out to the neighbors' to do their washing, I watch the baby, and Sevek takes care of Father. He's very sick, and Sevek buys medicine for him in the drugstore. I wondered where he got the money from. He told me that he helped unload the wagons that came to the stockrooms in the back yard. I was surprised. After all, he couldn't make any more than a few pennies at best! Now, when I heard you, I understood. Sevek put your pennies and his together and bought Father's medicine. But he isn't a crook!" Estusha burst into tears again, her whole body shuddering.

Shimek rose and went up to Estusha. He opened his mouth as if he wanted to say something, but the words failed him. Suddenly he bent his head, and he too burst into tears. For a little while he stood there, bewildered. Finally he said to Estusha in a strangled voice, "Estusha, I beg you, don't tell Sevek anything about this! And don't tell him that we know the truth. Do you promise?"

Estusha nodded. Then she left us and ran off.

We continued to give Sevek the pennies we collected during the week. Sevek took the money, and every Tuesday and Friday evening we sat under the chestnut tree and heard him tell the story of the movie, though we knew he hadn't set foot in the movie house.

Two weeks later, his father got well and we saw him sitting at the window. After another week we noticed him at the gate of our house. His wooden leg was stretched out before him, and he was leaning on his stand and selling cigarettes again.

One evening we were all sitting in the yard, at the foot of the chestnut tree. Sevek addressed us.

"Fellows, I've told you more than once about my dream to be a motion-picture director. Now I've written a scenario, my very first scenario. I can tell you about it. Do you want to hear?"

"Of course. Tell us!" we exclaimed.

"It's not a movie about Winatoo," said Sevek, "and it's not about Sherlock Holmes or Arsène Lupin or sheriffs and bandits. The plot of the movie isn't thrilling or tense, but it's very moving. Here is the story: There's this gang of kids who didn't have the means to buy a ticket to the movies. What did they do? They picked one of their bunch, saved their pennies, and gave him the money to buy a ticket. In exchange, the boy told them about the movies, down to the very last detail. One day the boy's father got sick and there wasn't a penny in the house. The boy tried to make some money unloading wagons, but the few cents he earned weren't enough. He racked his brains to find a way to make some money, and in the end he did the only thing he could. He took the money he'd got from his friends and bought medicine for his father. He didn't go to the movies anymore, but when he met with his friends he made up all kinds of stories. In his heart he sensed that his friends saw through his deception but were pretending not to notice. For this he was deeply grateful to them, but he didn't know how to thank them. Finally he decided he would tell them the truth, he would reveal the whole thing to them."

Sevek stopped a minute, as if to take a breath, and then he went on. "And in fact that's what he did. And that will be more or less the end of the movie. You can say your kind of movie is different, with daring deeds of heroism, noble heroes risking their necks! I thought about that a lot, but I asked myself, *Is it true that only the one who fires the pistol is the hero and only the one who risks his neck is noble?* Maybe the hero can also be a child who wanted to save his father's life and had no choice but to do things that were against his better nature? Can you imagine how that child must have felt, returning from the meetings with his friends in which he deluded them and fed them ridiculous yarns? Can you hear him crying at night? And his friends, who knew everything and kept quiet and went on giving him the pennies they worked so hard to save—weren't they noble? When I thought about it that way, I realized that thrilling stories don't have to take place on the lone prairie. Even our yard can serve as the stage for great deeds."

A thick silence stood between us. Our throats were stifled. Then Shimek said, "That will be a really fine movie! When you grow up, you can be sure they'll show it in the movie house. And when I'm a coachman I'll drive people there in my carriage. Can you imagine? I'll ride around in a carriage all the time!"

"And I," said Kubah, "I'll be there, in the theater, going down the aisles with my keg and selling ice cream. And whenever I have a mind to, I'll eat all the ice cream I want!"

"And if a fire breaks out at the movies," said Edek, "I'll gallop on a white horse in front of the fire truck, with a gleaming copper helmet on my head!"

"And I," I said, "will write it all down in a book."

Many years have passed since then. We grew up and our ways parted. I don't know if my friends' dreams came true. As for me, I kept my promise.

A SAD STORY

Esther, Sevek's little sister, was my age. We boys of the yard affectionately nicknamed her Estusha. She was a skinny girl with blue eyes and black hair, which she wore in two braids. Estusha wasn't the only girl in the yard, but we never showed any interest in girls; it never occurred to us to let them play with us. Neither in our football games, in which we used an old sock filled with dirt, nor in our games of sliding on the ice or cops and robbers. The girls lived in a world of their own. Every one of them kept a diary in which her playmates wrote doting rhymes. They had all sorts of dolls, cheap ones made of rags and more expensive ones that could open and close their eyes. Some of the girls collected what they called "gold," but which was really shiny candy wrappers. Others collected pretty buttons. We boys looked down on the girls and their diversions.

One day I went to visit Sevek. Estusha let me in.

"Sevek isn't at home," she told me. "Father sent him to the factory to get cigarettes." Sevek frequently used to run errands, since his father had a wooden leg.

"Mother isn't at home either," said Estusha. "She's doing the neighbors' washing, as usual. Won't you come in? I'm lonely here all by myself."

Estusha's invitation threw me into confusion. After all, we believed we would lose face if we played with girls! Her blue eyes looked at me in mute supplication. I couldn't refuse. I went in, and soon we were sitting at the table, playing chess. After a few moves, I was surprised. I was good at chess (in the last tournament I had been proclaimed champion of the yard), but now I became aware that Estusha was a serious opponent. She knew how to plan her moves prudently and wisely, playing a better game than most of the boys.

As we were playing and Estusha was considering her next move, I glanced at her face. It was pale and smooth as white marble. Her mouth was small and round, and her white teeth bit her lower lip tensely. Having decided, she moved the piece she was holding and threw me a glance. Suddenly I felt my heart leap. She had eyes like the sky on a lovely spring day. Large, wide open, and brilliant. I sat riveted to my seat, looking into her eyes, until she called me to attention.

"Well, it's your turn now. Why don't you move?"

I lowered my eyes. "I'm thinking," I said. I actually moved one of the pieces, but from that moment on I was unable to concentrate on the game. My gaze was not drawn to the chessboard but to Estusha's eyes. They overwhelmed me. They made me shiver in a strange way.

On account of Estusha's eyes, I lost the game. It was my first defeat in a long while. I, a boy, the chess champion of the yard, had been beaten by a girl! But I wasn't sorry. In my secret heart I was even glad I'd lost. Of course when I first heard Estusha announce "Checkmate!" I felt disappointed, as would any player who has been defeated in competition, but Estusha's announcement was accompanied by a look that compensated for my defeat. Her beautiful eyes were radiant, her pale face smiled. I, despite my defeat, rejoiced in the light of her eyes, the joy in her face.

That night, in bed, I thought about my visit with Estusha. Her company was good for me. I was ashamed to admit to myself that

I preferred playing with her to running around after a football with the boys. Little by little I dozed off, thinking of Estusha, and as I sank into sleep it seemed to me I was sinking into the deep, soothing blue of her eyes.

From then on I found all sorts of excuses for going to Sevek's house, hoping to see his sister. I never told Sevek about my game of chess with Estusha, and since Sevek never mentioned the matter to me I assumed that Estusha hadn't disclosed anything to him either. The hour we spent together, Estusha and I, had become our secret, to be shielded from the eyes of strangers.

During my visits Estusha was usually at home, but she pretended not to notice me. Upon my arrival she would withdraw to some corner and occupy herself with her own affairs. Every once in a while our glances met, and we spoke without a word.

Sevek didn't perceive what was going on. It surely never occurred to him that I was watching him and that every time I saw him go out on one of his father's errands, with the big satchel in his hand, I would slip into his house and play with Estusha. Sometimes it was checkers, sometimes chess, and sometimes I told her about the books I'd read. Estusha knew how to listen well. Her blue eyes prompted me to speak, and my words poured out unrestrained.

At night, in bed, I would think of Estusha. With my eyes open, staring into the darkness, I dreamed that we were on a ship and all at once a storm broke out. The ship sank, and I was swimming in the foaming sea, rescuing Estusha and bringing her to a desert island. On the island there were wild animals and cannibals, but I fought bravely, killing the wild beasts and thwarting every enemy plot.

It was good to dream. It let me forget that I didn't know how to swim, that I was afraid of Rex, the dog that belonged to Uncle Gedalyah's doorman, of Stashek, our own doorman's helper, and of every policeman who walked the streets with a pistol in his belt.

Estusha's eyes inspired me with courage and lent wings to my imagination.

It was for her sake that I dreamed of being a hero. For her sake I wanted to be better than I was. I aspired to kindle a spark of admiration in her blue eyes. In the morning, I awoke to the sound of a bird warbling in the branches of the chestnut tree, and the song was beautiful and moving. At once I thought, *Is Estusha listening to the song too?* In the evening the setting sun was like a tremendous crimson wheel. At once I thought, *Is Estusha looking at the sunset too?*

As the days passed I was attracted to Estusha all the more. I could no longer keep it a secret. I stopped playing with the boys in the yard and spent most of my time in Sevek's house. I had my fill of humiliations. I was an outcast among my friends. They had a name for me: "The Bridegroom." Estusha told me that her friends had also taken to calling her "The Bride." I lovingly accepted it all. One look of her eyes was enough to pay me back for all the insults I suffered. One laugh of Estusha's, which brought a blush to her pale cheeks, was enough to warm my heart.

In reality, Estusha's cheeks were always pale. Estusha was ill. Two years before, when she was eight, she had had pneumonia. She'd been bedridden for many days, but even after her recovery her temperature didn't go down. The doctor later diagnosed that she was suffering from tuberculosis.

In those days there were no effective medicines such as we have now. The doctor said that she had to drink a lot of milk, eat meat, and above all spend time in the country, in the fresh air. Sevek's family was poor. His father never made enough money. It was to no avail that he dragged himself around with his wooden leg, knocking on the stairs, begging the kindness of various charities. He found no sympathetic listeners.

It was then that my friend Shimek's mother, Geetl, went into action. She was a virtuous woman with a heart of gold. One morning she went from one apartment to the next in our yard, collecting donations. Every neighbor was to contribute as much as his generosity would allow. The money would enable Estusha to be sent to a sanatorium in Otwock, a town about forty kilometers from our city.

The tenants in our yard had little money, but when they heard Geetl's story they couldn't let her go away empty-handed. In the evening Geetl went to Sevek's parents, put a bundle of money on the table, and said, "Estusha is going to Otwock tomorrow!"

Sevek's mother hugged Geetl and kissed her. His father bent his head and was still. I learned all this from Estusha the next day as we said goodbye on the staircase, before she left for the sanatorium. Oh, how I wanted to escort her to the train! But I didn't dare.

"Goodbye, Estusha!" I said. Suddenly I put out my hands and gripped her shoulders, and my lips clung to her cheek. That was the first time I kissed a girl.

"Will you write to me?" asked Estusha.

Before I could answer her, Sevek appeared beside us. I ran down the stairs, burst out into the yard, and buried my face in the trunk of the chestnut tree.

Estusha stayed two months in the sanatorium. Every week I wrote her a letter. I'll never forget the first one I wrote. In those days we used a pen dipped in ink, and no matter how careful I was I repeatedly spoiled the writing with an ugly stain. I copied the letter ten times before I was satisfied.

It was the first letter I had ever written. I wanted to write many terms of endearment, all the fine words that thronged in my heart, but I was bashful. So in my letter I told her about the boys of the yard, the tricks we played in school. It was a one-way correspondence, since in my first letter I asked Estusha not to write me. I was afraid of the derision of my friends, who undoubtedly would take note of any letters that arrived. Estusha had no need to be afraid of derision. After all, no one knew her in the sanatorium.

The more I wrote to Estusha the freer I felt from inhibitions. I was even so bold as to end every letter with the words, "Do you remember how we parted, Estusha?" alluding to the kiss I'd given her.

I missed her very much. More than once in writing to her I was overcome by passion, and a tear dropped from my eyes and left a stain on the page. At first I took the trouble to copy the letter over, but as time went on I let the tear stains remain. Estusha would read those tears as if they were words.

Estusha returned from the sanatorium on a Friday morning, while I was in school. When I came home, I saw her at the gate. She was waiting for me. Her face was tanned, which emphasized the blue of her eyes all the more. I stood and looked at her. I wanted to say something, but I was too excited to utter a word. It was not until evening that I knocked on her door. We played checkers and chess, but Sevek was with us all the while and we couldn't talk. Only our eyes conversed.

Estusha's tan was deceptive. True, she had recovered somewhat in the sanatorium and even had gained a little weight, but her illness was not cured. The tuberculosis remained in her body. In time her tan faded, and her cheeks grew pale again. In the evenings her temperature went up, and then her cheeks bloomed like two roses.

The doctor forbade her to go to school. As the days passed and her condition became more severe, he ordered her to rest and nothing else.

Estusha lay by the window that looked out on the nearby roofs. As far as the eye could see were faded walls—no greenery, not a single bird. I don't know if Estusha knew how serious her illness was, but all the tenants of the yard whispered that her condition was critical.

Every day I visited her and sat for hours at her bedside. As her condition worsened, her face shriveled until it was like a bird's. Only the blue eyes retained their radiance.

I brought her books to read and told her stories. Some were true and some I made up. I never came empty-handed. Every day I brought Estusha flowers, which I would arrange in the clay jars that stood on the windowsill.

Where did I get the flowers? There was a flower store on the Christian street at the far end of our quarter, but I, a boy of ten, had no money. To get flowers I had to undergo an adventure fraught with danger.

Not far from our house was a city park with flower beds enclosed by fences. It was forbidden to walk in the flower beds. They were guarded by a watchman, a huge gentile who walked about the park keeping an eye on whatever went on in his realm. My desire to get the flowers for Estusha got the better of my fears. Every day I went to the park, sat by the gate on a bench next to a flower bed, and followed the watchman with my eyes. As soon as I saw him move away to the other side of the park, I jumped over the fence, and picked a handful of flowers. My whole body quaked the first time. As the days passed, my fears were allayed a bit. Several times the watchman noticed me and chased me. I fled for my life, as if a wild beast were racing at my heels. Only once did the watchman catch me, and the bruises left by his pointed stick remained on my back for many days. He hit me in the face too. When I returned from the park, I hid the flowers in a niche in the stairwell before I entered my house. Seeing my face, my mother screamed, "Great heavens! How did you get hurt?"

"I fell," I mumbled.

My mother washed my face, put iodine on it, and wrapped it in a cold, wet bandage. I kept still, not telling her about my bruised back, which hurt and burned. I accepted it all, for the flowers, still hidden in the niche, would put joy in Estusha's heart!

As Estusha's health weakened, my friends stopped tormenting me. They no longer teased me. They no longer called me "The Bridegroom," no longer regarded me as an outcast. On the contrary, I felt a certain sympathy in their glances. More than once it seemed as if they wanted to discuss Estusha with me, but something stopped them.

Sevek, who had been my first and foremost mocker, clung to me as a brother. One day, at twilight, he came to me. My parents were not at home. I thought that Sevek had come for a chat or a game, as usual, but all at once he burst into tears. He stood in the doorway, sobbing loudly.

"What happened, Sevek?" I asked.

Sevek couldn't manage to answer me. It was only when he calmed down that he could speak.

"The doctor called on us today. After he left, I heard Mother and Father whispering. Estusha's days are numbered!" He burst into tears again. I cried too, unrestrained. Finally Sevek said, "You must never let Estusha on to this. You have to pretend you know nothing."

Sevek left and I ran out to the park. My eyes were blind with tears. It was a wonder the watchman didn't catch me. Returning home, I took my one and only treasure, my stamp album, and went over to Sevek's house.

"What beautiful flowers!" Estusha exclaimed. "Maybe now at last you'll tell me where you get them?"

"My cousin opened a flower shop," I answered. "He's happy to give me the leftover flowers."

"And what's that?" asked Estusha, seeing the album in my hand.

"A present for you," I said and bent over her bed, offering her my treasure.

Estusha put out her hands. I assumed she wanted to take the album, but she gripped my head and drew it down to her breast.

Through her pink gown I felt the warmth of her body. I could hear her heartbeats fluttering like a bird imprisoned in her breast.

I raised my head. Estusha smiled and said, "Well, let's have a game of chess."

We set up the board and began the game. After a little while Estusha cried, "I want you really to play!"

"But I *am* playing!"

"No! You're letting me win!"

The truth was that, wishing to please her, I had been playing an intentionally careless game. A few times, when Estusha's head was turned for a minute, I'd remove one of my bishops or pawns, sure she was unaware of what I was doing. As it turned out, I was wrong.

"What do you mean?" I held my own. "Is it my fault that you're a good player? Don't you remember our first game? You won then too! When you get well, Estusha, we'll hold a tournament and you'll be queen of the yard, the champion at chess!"

"When I get well," Estusha whispered. Her blue eyes were veiled in mist.

That night Estusha hemorrhaged and was taken to the hospital. The next day Sevek told me her condition was grave.

My days passed in numbness. My nights were without sleep. "Heal her, O God, I beseech thee," I prayed in the dark. I prayed and felt that no one was listening. Was it possible that the walls of my room were obstructing my prayer? I got up and opened the window. The sky stretched above, twinkling with myriad stars. Who knows? Perhaps the stars were the souls of children who had died before their time. Would Estusha become a star? Was it possible that she would see me from above, and twinkle at me and I wouldn't know?

Estusha died a week later. Her feeble body could struggle no more.

All the tenants in the yard went to the funeral. I stayed home. I felt I couldn't go. I was afraid I'd break down.

For a long while I lay in bed, burying my face in the pillow. In the end I went down to the yard and sat under the chestnut tree. Just then I saw a dead bird there. It must have fallen from the tree. Its wings were spread open, and its tiny beak seemed to be crying for help.

I bent down and with my hands dug a little hole in the ground next to the tree trunk, a grave for the bird. I took it in my arms, kissed it on the head, and felt the soft plumage caressing my lips. Then I laid it down in the hole and covered it with earth. A little mound remained.

I didn't cry. I didn't have the strength to cry.

THE DESERT ISLAND

It all began with books.

Our yard was a gloomy one, shut in on all sides by gray, faded houses. It enclosed us like a shell. The books we read gave us a glimpse of the wide world outside. They liberated our imaginations. They enabled us to embark on long voyages, crossing deserts, galloping over the plains, participating in heroic escapades. It was no wonder we liked to read.

Every one of our group had a few books, which passed from hand to hand until we came to know them all. Sevek was the first to join the library, followed by Shimek, Kubah, and Edek. For fifty cents a month they were entitled to take out one book a day. I envied them.

One day I said to my father, "I need fifty cents."

"What for?"

"I want to join the library. I want to read," I answered.

"Aren't there enough signs in the street, by the shops? You can read them! There's no need to waste fifty cents."

I pleaded with him, and in the end I managed to convince him. I was given fifty cents to join the library. Every day from then on I ran over to the cellar apartment on the next street where the librarian, a humpbacked, bespectacled young man, fulfilled my requests and lent me books by Jules Verne and Karl May.

My evenings were engrossed in reading. I couldn't tear myself away from the books. Father would say, "It's a waste of kerosene," and put out the lamp. But as soon as my parents had fallen asleep I put on the light again, and more than once I dozed off with my face buried in a book and the lamp still burning—only to catch it the next morning from my father.

"The devil's gotten into you," my father would scold me. "I wish you would tell me what you find in those books! Why, there's nothing in them but doubletalk and nonsense!"

But Father's reprimands did not chill my enthusiasm. The more I read the more I was drawn to books.

It really was the devil in me.

We didn't stop at reading. The characters in the books enchanted us. We wanted to copy them and be their very image. Was it possible that only Karl May's Indians knew how to shoot an arrow and throw a lasso, and only the pathfinders, Cooper's heroes, knew how to follow a trail? We were positive that if we practiced we could work the same wonders they did.

We devoted many hours to practice. In the city park we would follow footprints in the soft earth of the paths. Every shoe had a shape of its own. One had a big, pointed tip; another had a narrow heel; a third had a rubber sole whose grooves were prominent in the earth, like a wavy drawing. When we managed to catch up with the person we were trailing, our joy knew no bounds. So it was that we became pathfinders.

And crack archers as well. We stole the wooden hoops from the barrels that were brought to the stockrooms in the back yard. Every hoop was cut in two, so we had bows. We used a cord for the string and made the arrows out of heavy iron wire, with a sharp point. Armed with our bows and arrows, we would go out to the yard, hang a wooden board marked with a black circle on the trunk of the chestnut tree, and hold target practice.

Sevek was the leading pathfinder of our group. Shimek was the champion archer. I became an expert with the lasso. I got hold of a long rope, made a loop at one end of it, and would wind the rope on my arm and fling it with a flick of my hand. My targets were the back of a chair or the edge of a cupboard. After a while I set my heart on a real target and focused my activities on my sister Sarenka, who was three years my junior. I used to wait in ambush for her behind the door. When she entered the room, I would let my lasso fly, and the noose would tighten about her neck.

Sarenka would protest loudly. At times she burst into tears and threatened to tell on me to Father. And I, fearing his response, had to appease her and let her play with the lasso, though she didn't even know how to wind it properly.

My days with the lasso soon came to an end.

One day I was waiting in ambush for Sarenka. When the door opened, I threw the lasso, and the noose tightened around Eli, Uncle Nachum's eldest son. At first Eli let out a startled yelp, but when he saw me with the end of the rope in my hand he smacked me loudly twice, freed his neck of the noose, and poured out his wrath on me.

"You murderer! You want to hang someone? The next time I see you with a rope in your hand, I'll break your bones!"

Eli confiscated my lasso. You might think I made myself a new one, but it wasn't so! Eli, a hotheaded fellow, was a regular guest in our house, and he'd given me a taste of his punishment more than once. His threat had the desired effect. Since that incident I took care never to touch a rope again.

I gave up the lasso, but I never took my mind off books and their tales of wonder. I gave them a lot of thought, and at night I would dream about their heroes. I accompanied the courageous

Indians on their hunting trips, the discoverers of new lands on their daring voyages. Oh, how I wanted to grow up! I wouldn't stay in our miserable yard. The world was wide and open. True, it was populated with many heroes already, but there would be a place for me too!

Since we weren't grown up yet, we had to make do with mere dreams and games. In our games we were Indians on the endless prairies or Captain Grant's children, submarine commanders or balloon pilots. We adopted names for ourselves too, such as Winatoo, Old Shaterhend, Sherlock Holmes, and the like.

One day Sevek came to me. By the look on his face I could see he was about to let me in on something important. He summoned me to the yard. Once we were seated in the shade of the chestnut tree, he told me his secret.

"Listen," he said. "I'm sick of games. I've decided to be a real Robinson Crusoe. And you, Benny, will be Friday."

I froze with wonder. "Where will you get a boat?" I asked. "How will you sail it? And where are you going to find a desert island?"

"I've thought of everything," said Sevek. "We'll use the lake in the park."

My eyes opened wide at those words.

At the far end of the Jewish quarter was a city park, a green, shady spot unique among the walls of the houses. In the middle of the park was a lake with two white swans. In the center of the lake was a tiny island with a few bushes and a weeping willow bent over the water. More than once we had watched the swans emerge from the water and climb the shore of the island, where they would stand, craning their long necks and waving their white wings like enormous fans.

At last we too had happened upon a desert island. It was actually within our grasp. But how could we reach it?

"Do you have a boat?" I asked.

"It all began with an old wooden washtub that I found in the back yard," Sevek told me. "It's a long time now since I decided to get to the island in the lake and live there like Robinson Crusoe. But I didn't know how to cross the lake. When I saw the wash-tub, I made up my mind. This is the boat that I'll sail to the island!"

Just then I had a vision of the park watchman, a mean gentile whose mere shadow cast terror upon us. "And what about the watchman?" I asked.

"Who told you we were going to sail during the day?" replied Sevek. "You know, at ten o'clock at night the watchman blows his whistle, and after everyone has left he locks the gates. We'll hide in the bushes till the watchman leaves, and then we'll sail to the island."

"And how will we get back home? After all, the gates to the park are locked at night!"

"We'll climb the iron bars on the park fence."

Sevek had thought of everything and had planned the operation down to the last detail. There was nothing for me to do but admire his resourcefulness.

I still had my doubts, however. "Have you told the others?"

"No," replied Sevek. "I decided to share the secret with you alone. The fewer people involved, the better our chances will be."

"What if the washtub tips over?" I asked. "After all, we don't know how to swim!"

"Take a bundle of straw with you," Sevek merrily declared.

"What do you mean?"

"Haven't you heard the saying, 'A drowning man grasps at straws'?" Sevek burst out laughing.

Then and there we fixed the date—the following Tuesday. But one problem remained: how could we explain our absence from home for an entire night? Sevek had thought of that too. We would tell our families we were going on a school trip. Our class was sailing down the river to a nearby resort and returning the following day.

And in fact that was what I did. I lied to my parents. I was ten years old; how else could I get away?

As the date of our voyage drew near, we made tense preparations. I asked my friends to lend me some personal articles that I could use as equipment. I took Shimek's rusty pocketknife and Edek's spyglass, which was broken and without lenses. On Tuesday evening, when Sevek whistled for me, I said a quick goodbye to my parents and ran out to the yard.

We waited until it was dark and then slipped out to the back yard. In a corner between two stockrooms, we found our boat, the wooden washtub. We carried it between us and set off for the park. At the gate we stopped a minute and tried to catch a glimpse of the watchman. He was out of sight, so we went in and hid in a thicket of bushes. We sprawled there, waiting.

Before leaving home I'd stuck a piece of charcoal in my pocket. Now, as I sprawled among the bushes in the dark, I took out the charcoal and smeared my face till it was black. Sevek didn't know I planned to blacken my face, and he hadn't seen me do it.

At last we heard a whistle. The watchman went through the park and rounded up the visitors like a shepherd driving his flock. We heard faint voices, a sharp laugh, a child crying. Then everything was still. The watchman locked the gates and disappeared.

We peeked out. The park lamps were turned off, but the moon, which had risen in the sky, spread its pale light over everything. We darted out from our hiding place, lugging the washtub. Just then Sevek glanced at me. He was so surprised at the sight of my black face that he let go of the washtub, which fell and landed on my toes. We both let out a shout, Sevek in amazement and I in pain.

"What's that?" asked Sevek.

"Friday be black, master," I answered.

Sevek burst into a mighty laugh. I rubbed my injured foot and groaned aloud.

"Okay, Friday, stop your wailing!" Sevek ordered.

We approached the lake. The full moon was reflected in it like a silver disk. The weeping willow on our desert island seemed to be reaching out to us. Near the opposite bank we saw two white spots, the pair of swans drifting over the water.

Little by little we lowered the washtub into the water. Sevek got in first and put out a hand to me. The washtub started to rock beneath me, and my heart pounded. In another minute we were sailing to the island, rowing with our hands as oars.

At last we set foot on the island. It was twenty paces long and fifteen wide. This was the piece of land we had dreamed of, and now we were its sole inhabitants!

Sevek pulled the washtub up the sloping shore. From that moment on, Sevek was not only my friend and companion. He was Robinson Crusoe, my master.

"Friday," he commanded me, "light a fire!"

"Friday forget matches, master," I replied.

"You numskull! Since when does Robinson Crusoe use matches? Take two stones and rub them together till you make a spark!"

"Friday do it, master," I replied. I took two stones and rubbed them together for a long while, but to no avail. There was no spark.

"We'll have to skip that," said Sevek. "I forgot that the cannibals sailing their boats in the sea might detect the fire. The flames would give us away. We'd better put up a shelter."

"Where, master?"

"In the shade of the willow tree," said Sevek.

In a little while we were sitting under the weeping willow. Its bending branches enclosed us like a hut. Through the leaves we saw the surface of the lake and, on the horizon, beyond the trees in the park, the flickering windows of the houses. A chill extended from the water and a damp smell from the ground.

The sky grew thick with clouds, which hid the moon. Then lightning flashed and thunder pealed. I went down on my knees, beating my brow on the ground.

"What's wrong with you, Friday?" asked Sevek.

"Friday scared, master," I replied. "Friday ask mercy from thunder god and lightning god."

"Once a savage always a savage, Friday," Sevek chided me. "How many times have I told you there are no gods like that! There is only one God in Heaven and we must pray to Him alone. Can't you get that into your head, you moron?"

"Friday already dressed, master," I said. "Why put more on?"

Sevek didn't get to answer me. At that moment there was a cloudburst, and it began to pour.

"We get out of here, master!" I yelled.

"Where are we going to go, Friday?" Sevek replied. "We haven't built our permanent quarters yet."

For a minute Sevek was at a loss. Then he exclaimed, "Come on, let's get the washtub and hold it over our heads like an umbrella!"

"Master know everything," I said and dashed through the willow branches to the shore. When I got there my heart sank. The washtub was gone! It must have slid down the wet slope and slipped into the water. I strained my eyes. In the flash of lightning that tore through the canopy of clouds and illuminated the surrounding area for an instant, I made out the washtub floating far off on the water of the lake.

"Boat run away, master!" I yelled.

Sevek stood at my side, bewildered. "It doesn't matter if we get wet in the rain," he said, "but how are we going to get off this island?"

I took Edek's spyglass from my pocket and carefully examined the surface of the water.

"What's that?" Sevek said in surprise.

"Friday look at sea, master," I said. "Maybe comes a boat?"

"Very smart!" Sevek scowled. "Robinson Crusoe stayed on his island for twenty-eight years before a ship came to take him home. And you, Friday, expect to be saved after only one hour!"

It continued raining in torrents. We were drenched. But we kept up our vigil on the shore, eyeing the lake. The washtub rocked lightly on the water, at times drawing closer, at times moving farther away.

"If it doesn't stop raining, our boat will fill up with water and sink," said Sevek.

"And we not go back home, master!" I wailed.

Fortunately for us, the rain stopped. The sky cleared. Moonbeams broke through the clouds, and the lake winked at us with its smooth, silvery water. The lights in the distant windows went out one after the other. It was late at night.

We sat on the island shore and followed the washtub with our eyes. My whole body was shivering. My teeth chattered from the cold. The night closed in on us like a wall. From the lake we could hear the croaking of frogs. Somewhere in the distance a dog was barking. From the tops of the trees that stood like sentinels about the lake, birds screeched strangely. We were frightened.

We sat where we were, listening to the sounds of the night. The moon withdrew behind the canopy of clouds again, and it was dark as pitch. My heart quaked in fear. I moved closer to Sevek, seeking refuge and shelter, and I felt him trembling too.

Just then we heard a thumping noise behind us. We shuddered. We pricked up our ears. Our flesh creeped in terror as we heard the sound again, followed by odd, rhythmic thumps.

I grabbed Sevek's hand and didn't let go. For a while we sat in a hush, listening to each other's heartbeats. Then all at once Sevek turned around, broke into a mighty laugh, and pointed at something. "Look!" he cried.

Set off by the bushes that blackened across from us like a dark smudge, I made out the pair of swans. They stood one next to the other, beating their wings powerfully.

"Damn it!" Sevek cursed. "Two miserable swans have scared Robinson Crusoe!" And he bent over, picked up some pebbles, and threw them at the swans. I followed him. I threw stones with a vengeance, making up for the moments of terror I'd gone through. The startled swans slid down the slope into the lake and fled.

Once again we were sitting on the shore, under the weeping willow, shivering in the cold.

"Go over the island, Friday," said Sevek, "and examine it well. You may find the footprints of cannibals in the sand."

I didn't budge. "Friday freeze," I said. "Friday scared of dark, master."

Sevek made no response.

The minutes crawled by like hours. When would the dawn rise? Would this night ever end? I remembered my warm room, my soft bed, and a sigh escaped my lips.

"It's hard to be Robinson Crusoe," Sevek responded with a sigh, "harder than I thought."

I wanted to answer him, but my eyes had closed. A minute later, before I fell asleep, I heard Sevek snoring.

We sat there in a deep sleep all that night, leaning back on the trunk of the weeping willow. We awoke suddenly.

A chill wind pierced us to the bone. Our clothes were as wet as if we'd taken a dip in the lake. We shivered. Every part of our bodies hurt. For a minute we sat and stared around us. The cloud banks hovering in the eastern sky had turned pink. It was dawn.

We jumped up. Where was our washtub? The lake stretched out before us. We saw nothing but the swans on the surface of the water, white swans craning their long necks and looking angrily at us. Was it possible that they remembered the shower of stones with which we greeted them when they came to keep us company on the desert island?

"The washtub sank, Sevek!" I shouted. In my consternation I forgot that he was my master and I had to address him as such.

Sevek didn't lose his head. He dashed over to the other side of the island, and I ran after him. What I saw there gave me a new lease on life.

The washtub was stuck in the dirt on the shore. The dawn breeze rippled on the water, which half filled it.

Sevek jumped down and held on to the side of the washtub as if he were afraid it would slip out of his hands again. In no time we were bending over it, bailing out the water with rusty cans we found on the island.

"We have to hurry," said Sevek. "The watchman will be coming to the park soon."

With the washtub at our disposal again, I resumed my whimsical tone. "Friday not scared, master. Us make it."

And so we did.

We set sail, leaving the desert island behind us. We rowed powerfully with our hands. On shore we hid in the thicket of bushes. In a little while we heard the grating sound of the park gate. From our hiding place we saw the watchman begin to make the rounds of the paths, picking up papers with his stick. We waited until the first visitors appeared in the park. Then we slipped out of the thicket and set off for home.

"We tell fellows, master?" I asked.

"No, Friday," replied Sevek. "They might plan the same adventure one day themselves. Better let them learn by experience that it's hard to be Robinson Crusoe. Harder than people imagine."

DAVID AND GOLIATH

At the end of the Day of Atonement, our fathers would begin building a sukkah, the booth for the Sukkoth holiday. A chilly autumn wind shook the upper branches of the chestnut tree in the yard, but our hearts swelled with warmth as if spring had arrived. We knew that the most beautiful holiday of all was soon to come.

Our fathers were quick to start building the sukkah, but we boys of the yard were quicker. By the end of summer we had already gone over the yard, gathering boards and planks. Our fathers planted the first peg of the sukkah, and we began where they left off. The next morning we took stock of the materials we had collected in the yard and then got down to the construction of the sukkah. Sevek was the supervisor and we were his assistants, holding the corner posts straight, passing him the planks and nails. By noon four walls stood in the yard, without a roof or door. The planks were bare and warped and dotted with cracks.

The main task was still before us. We labored from dawn to dusk, getting the decorations ready. We worked as a team, never going to bed on time, but our parents weren't strict with us. They smiled, seeing the enthusiasm that gripped us.

We knew that for eight days straight the sukkah would be our enchanted castle. Our fathers would fulfill their obligation by eating in the sukkah, and we would stay and play in it throughout the days and evenings. After all, we had built and decorated it with our own hands, and now it was beautiful and captivating. Its walls were covered with rugs. Lamps, baskets, paper chains, and all kinds of fruit dangled from its ceiling of greenery, and its floor was padded with mats. We children, who lived in stifling apartments, loved the sukkah, with its ceiling of leaves and branches through which the stars winked at us and its prevailing autumn wind that caressed our faces.

Eight days of festivity. Eight days of joy.

If it were not for Stashek, Antony the doorman's helper, the festive joy would have been complete.

Antony had spent most of his life among Jews, and he was well acquainted with the habits and customs of the tenants in the yard. When he came to our house to put out the lamp on Sabbath eves, he was served a glass of brandy and a big slice of white Sabbath bread. Then he would remove his hat and express his thanks, seasoning his Polish with a few words of faulty Yiddish, which brought a smile to our lips. The tenants of the yard used to whisper among themselves, "If only all gentiles were like our Antony!"

It was not so with Stashek, who had the face of a deceiver and whose ailing eyes had a decidedly evil cast. From the time he was a child he had picked on the Jewish children in the yard. He made them miserable as he persecuted them, frightening them with the dead mice he hid in his pocket, stealing or appropriating their paltry toys, and hitting them as well. In the morning he would charge out of his house, his hands stuck in the pockets of his shabby pants and his eyes darting in search of a victim. Seeing him, the group of children at their games would retreat to a far corner of the yard, but he would walk straight up to them, teasing them and sticking out his long tongue, pulling at them and punching. The children would flee in tears. At the sound of their screams Antony the doorman would appear, having awakened from his nap after a night on watch at the gate. Seeing Stashek at his tricks again, he would grab him by the scruff of his neck, remove the belt from his pants, and beat the young bully.

Such was Stashek's behavior as a child. In time, when he grew up, the evil look in his eyes grew sharper, and his stepfather no longer intimidated him. Now it was old Antony who feared the attack of the waif he had adopted. Tall and powerful, when Stashek walked about the yard no one stood in his way. It was not only the children he bullied, but the adults as well. Stashek knew that the mere sight of him was enough to strike terror in them, and this he enjoyed immensely.

The Jewish tenants of the yard were afraid of Stashek every day of the week, and even more so on Sundays. That was the day, the Christian Sabbath, when Stashek would invite his cronies over. They would get drunk and go out to the yard, screaming at the top of their lungs, and start a brawl. Stashek was the leader of the band. When he appeared in the yard wearing his high, shiny boots, the very picture of authority, we Jews cowered. Some would say, "Watch out for the villain!" and others would say, "That rat has a knife hidden in his boot. Heaven help whoever provokes him!"

The Sukkoth holiday was ushered in and cast its light on the faces of father and son alike. The sukkah was overflowing with splendor. The leafy ceiling swayed lightly in the wind, and the clear night outside adorned itself with a full moon. In the sukkah were tables made of boards covered with snow-white tablecloths, and the lit holiday candles added their glow to the shining bottles of wine. The faces of those seated at the table were radiant as well, making it hard to recognize them as belonging to ordinary weekday Jews, storekeepers and tradesmen with families to support.

We children sang the holiday songs and then grew silent and looked up at our fathers, who rose to say the blessing over the wine. And then—

Then Stashek came, the spiteful villain, and put an end to our holiday joy. Suddenly we heard a crash. The green ceiling cracked all at once. A cat came flying through the gap and landed on the table, breaking the plates, knocking the bottles over, and fleeing for its life, upending the candlesticks in its way. "Stashek!" shouted the guests, who rose in alarm and put out the fire that had taken hold of the tablecloth. The children began to howl. As they were screaming in fear, a torrent of water suddenly poured down from above, putting out the candles, spoiling the meal, and drenching us all. Before we could run for safety, the sukkah was bombarded with stones, which would have cracked our skulls had it not been for the leafy ceiling that broke their fall.

This was the work of Stashek, who would climb to the top of the stairs every Sukkoth eve, wait in ambush by the window that overlooked the yard, throw down a cat, pour water from the bucket in his hand, and fling stones. Outside, from the staircase window, came his loud, taunting laughter. "Hah hah hah!" Stashek had beaten the Jews, all of them!

Leizer, Sevek's father, would grab a wine bottle by its neck and wave it like a mace, ready to dash out and teach Stashek a lesson. But the neighbors would clutch at his sleeves, blocking his way, pleading, "Don't put your life in danger, Leizer! That rat Stashek has a knife hidden in his boot!"

The festivity was over. The paper lamps and colorful chains were dimmed. Our fathers returned shamefacedly to their places, straightened the tablecloth, held the wine glasses in their trembling hands, and mournfully finished the blessing that had been broken off. We children sat there, eyes lowered, as tears rolled down our cheeks and fell on the stained tablecloth.

This scene was repeated every year.

My father was a hefty Jew. He had broad shoulders and big muscles. Once I saw Father pick up a horseshoe that had fallen off the foot of a horse in the yard. He gripped it in his hand, and little by little he bent it and pressed the two ends together. I also remember the summer day when screams of terror startled everyone inside. We ran out to the back yard, where a horrible sight met our eyes. Among the stockrooms was a wagon loaded with boxes. Pinned beneath its wheels, in a pool of blood, was Moti, Kubah's little brother. The boy had dashed over from the yard, and the wagoner, not noticing him, had run him over. The people standing about were at a loss, with looks of consternation on their faces. But then Father crawled beneath the wagon until his whole body was engulfed between the wheels. He propped himself firmly on his hands and knees and began straightening his back. Little by little he rose. The heavy wagon was lifted, and the wheels hovered in space for a moment, just long enough for the people congregating about the wagon to extricate the child's bleeding body.

I was proud of my father, proud of his great strength. One night, home from the sukkah after our holiday had been spoiled by Stashek, Father sat at the table, his face pale, his head bowed, and his big, heavy-veined hands lying helplessly before him. My heart ached. Why didn't Father seek to avenge our desecrated holiday?

Father sensed what was going on inside me. He lowered his eyes and was silent. In the end I couldn't hold back. I blurted out a broken, impassioned plea.

"Father, why did you keep still? Why didn't you go out and get back at Stashek? Why, with your little finger you could have put a stop to him!"

Father lifted his sad eyes to me and said, "Son, we Jews should never provoke the gentiles. We are in exile. It is our misfortune to have lived out the verse, 'How should one chase a thousand and two put ten thousand to flight?' We Jews are under obligation to one another. If we take our revenge on one of the gentiles, the others immediately will join hands and come to slaughter us. No personal valor will save us. It is our punishment to suffer disgrace and endure these agonies."

"For how long, Father?"

"Till our righteous Messiah comes, son."

In my heart I rejected what my father said, but I didn't dare to differ with him. The words that struggled to reach my lips died away at the sight of Father's hands lying helplessly before him, and at the sight of his eyes clouded with grief.

Another year passed. Sevek was fourteen, we were twelve.

The day after Yom Kippur, we gathered as usual in the shade of the chestnut tree in the yard to plan the construction of our sukkah. Sevek brought a notebook and pencil.

"Fellows," said Sevek, "this year we're going to put up the most beautiful sukkah ever! I suggest we divide up the jobs before we get down to work—the planks and the decorations, the tools and the branches for the ceiling."

The group was in an uproar, each with his own proposals. Suddenly we heard Shimek the redhead's voice as he got up and silenced the others.

"And Stashek," said Shimek, "have you forgotten him? We'll build a sukkah and that louse will come and wreck it. So what's this talk about dividing up the jobs?"

"What do you want? What do you suggest?" asked Sevek crossly.

"Not to let him!" replied Shimek. "Five are stronger than one!"

"But how?"

"We have to think!"

"Maybe we can wait for Stashek on the staircase, in the dark?" Edek proposed. "If we all jump on him at once he won't be able to stand up to us."

Kubah seconded him. "We'll set an ambush for him and push him out the window. Let him fall down to the yard, the rat! He should break his bones!"

I kept still. I remembered my talk with my father, his sad eyes, his strong remarks.

Sevek also rose. He looked annoyed. There had always been

a latent rivalry between Shimek and Sevek, owing to Shimek's claim to the leader's crown. Now Sevek was offended by his rival's having taken the initiative; the words that burst from his mouth were derisive and angry.

"What Shimek said is just a lot of gibberish! We are children and Stashek is a big, strong gentile. Even if we have the nerve to jump on him and spoil his plans on the night of the holiday, the next day he'll pay us back twice over! It's easy to talk and pretend to be a hero, but when it comes down to action you can be sure we'll back out at the last minute. Shimek's proposal reminds me of the story about the cat and the mice."

Puzzled, we lowered our heads. Sevek went on.

"If you haven't heard the story, here it is. Once upon a time the mice held a meeting to decide how to put an end to the threat of the cat. One little mouse got up and said, 'I suggest we sneak up on the cat while he's napping and tie a bell to his neck. That way he won't be able to catch us any more, because the minute he comes close to us the bell will ring and warn us.' The mice listened to him and unanimously decided, 'This proposal of our younger member is brilliant. We shall do it!' But what happened? They couldn't find a mouse brave enough to go up to the sleeping cat and tie a bell to its neck."

"We're not mice!" Shimek muttered, and his lips quivered. "If we plan it all . . ."

Sevek interrupted him. "Look at the redhead, our hero! David, who fought with Goliath, was a redhead too. As the Bible says: 'He was ruddy, and had beautiful eyes.' Now, really, let us see *your* courage!"

Shimek was offended. He turned without a word and left the group. We sat in silence. Then Sevek opened his notebook and began writing.

"Who's going to take care of the planks? The decorations? The ceiling? The tools?"

During the next few days we got down to constructing the sukkah, and our hands were full. Shimek took no part in any of our activities. He apparently couldn't forget the insult. While we ran about our yard and the neighboring ones, searching for building materials, Shimek kept out of sight. It seemed the earth had opened its mouth and swallowed him. The day before the holiday we met Geetl, Shimek's mother, and asked her where Shimek was.

"He's been sick for three days now. He has severe headaches. Yesterday the doctor came and examined him, but he couldn't tell what the disease was. Today Shimek had a high fever, and we're very worried."

We were sorry about Shimek and the grudge that kept him from joining us. And we were sorrier about his illness, which would prevent him from celebrating with us in the sukkah.

The holiday spirit was in the air. From the windows came the sweet aromas of special dishes. Stashek walked through the yard, his ailing eyes squinting at the sukkah while an evil smile played about his lips.

It was a clear evening. The full moon sailed over the sky. We sat at the table, and the lit candles lent a cast of gold to the decorations. Our sukkah was elegant. It had been years since we'd put up such a beautiful sukkah.

We sat with our fathers and sang the holiday songs. As we intoned the melodies, our hearts squirmed in dread. We knew we wouldn't escape disgrace. The outrage would descend on us from the high staircase window. Doubtlessly that villain Stashek was already lurking there with the cat, the bucket of water, and the stones.

The singing stopped and we held our breath. Another minute, another instant . . .

All at once we heard a scream of terror outside. It was followed by an extended howl, like that of a wounded animal. The howl was so penetrating that all of us in the booth jumped up. We burst out to the yard.

The howling had broken out on the staircase. We went up and saw the body of a man stretched out beneath the window. In spite of the darkness we knew it was Stashek. There was a bucket of water beside him and a pile of stones on the windowsill. Could it have been Stashek who howled? Now he lay there on his back, still as a stone.

At once we seized him and carried him down to Antony the doorman's cellar apartment. Antony dashed out to us half-drunk, his eyes popping with fright. Stashek was placed on the couch by the door. Blood flowed from his forehead and covered his eyes.

"Call the Red Cross!" cried Marya, Antony's wife, who stood to one side, her face pale as a ghost, wringing her hands.

Within half an hour the car arrived. Two young men dressed in white robes jumped out, laid the fainting Stashek on a stretcher, and put him in the car. It sped out of the yard sounding its siren, taking Stashek to the hospital.

For a moment we stood outside, tongue-tied. Then we went back to the sukkah. As they said the blessing over wine, our fathers' faces were pale, and the cups shook in their hands. When our mothers appeared with their trays heaped with holiday delicacies, the tension lessened.

"Now the rat has got his punishment!" someone said.

"A thief will catch it in the end!"

"We have witnessed a Sukkoth miracle!"

"But who hit Stashek on the forehead?" asked Leizer, Sevek's father. The question hung in the air, unanswered.

Finally someone ventured an opinion. "Most likely the cat that Stashek was about to throw out the window scratched him on the forehead. Stashek was startled and fell, and as he fell he hit his head and lost consciousness."

"Yes," we agreed, "there's no doubt it was the cat that wounded the bully!"

At the end of the feast, voices rose in song again. It had been years since we'd sung that way. We sat in our sukkah in peace. Stashek no longer threatened us.

It was midnight when we left the sukkah. The candles burned out their last moments, and drops of tallow fell on the candlesticks. Outside, the night was clear and cold.

"Heroic cat!" we called out. "May you always be well and strong!"

By the next morning the cat was no longer alive. Antony the doorman agreed that it was the cat that had scratched Stashek and caused him to fall and suffer a brain concussion. He caught the cat and drowned it in a barrel of water in the back yard. We saw its corpse floating on the water.

We decided to visit Shimek to let him in on the previous night's experience, but Geetl, his mother, met us at the door with a worried look.

"Shimek has taken a turn for the worse," she said. "His temperature went up. Now it's 104."

"What does the doctor say?" we asked.

"The doctor was here this morning," replied Geetl, "but he still can't make a diagnosis."

Shimek's illness continued for several days. He lay there hour after hour with his eyes closed. At night he was delirious with fever. After a week his temperature went down, and soon Shimek recovered completely. He came back to us and joined our games again. His sickness had apparently taken his mind off the grudge he had held against Sevek. Still, Shimek was not the same. His face was very pale. Shimek withdrew into silence. Since he'd returned to us he hardly spoke.

One afternoon, we were playing in the city park. All at once we heard shouts. In the lane on the other side of the broad lawn a large bulldog raced, barking and baring its teeth. It must have snapped the doghouse chain and broken into the park. Now it was running wild and pouncing on everyone in its path.

David and Goliath · 107

The adults scattered. The children cried and shrieked. One boy tried to escape by climbing a tree, but the bulldog caught him and sank its teeth into his leg. The boy's screams echoed throughout the park and cast terror upon us.

As we were standing there petrified, the bulldog turned toward the lawn that separated it from us.

"Run for it!" commanded Sevek. He was the first to pick up his heels, with us right behind him. As we ran we looked back to see if the bulldog was chasing us. All at once our hearts froze.

Shimek was standing where we had been and the bulldog was running toward him. At that moment Shimek drew a slingshot from his pocket. Fitting a stone to it, he let it fly and hit the charging dog in the forehead. The bulldog's rush was halted. Shimek made the most of this and shot another stone and still another.

The big bulldog burst out howling, dropped its tail between its legs, made for the iron park gate, and vanished.

We followed the action breathlessly. Shimek walked up to us quietly, but in our amazement we were unable to utter a word.

Sevek suddenly struck his brow and fixed penetrating eyes on Shimek. "Since when do you have a slingshot?" he asked. "And where did you learn to shoot so well?"

Shimek was silent. His face, pale after his illness, grew paler still. In the end he said faintly, "Come on, fellows, let's go back to our chestnut tree. There's something I must tell you."

We sat in the shade of the tree. Shimek stood, leaning back on the trunk. He was silent for a moment, as if choosing his words. Then he said in a strangled voice, "I'm the one who wounded Stashek."

"But you got sick a few days before the holiday!" cried Kubah.

"And you had a high temperature!" added Edek.

"How did you hit Stashek without his noticing you?" I asked.

Only Sevek kept quiet. He looked at Shimek with penetrating eyes.

"Fellows," said Shimek, "maybe when I hit the bulldog with the slingshot I gave myself away, but that's not the reason I'm making this confession to you now. For days now Stashek has been lying in the hospital. True, the doctors say he'll get well eventually, but since it happened I felt I couldn't bear the terrible burden of my secret by myself. I need you, boys! But I'd better start at the beginning."

"Sit down, Shimek," said Sevek. "Tell us!"

Shimek sat down, folded his hands on his knees, and spoke with his head bent, as if he were telling his secret to the ground alone.

"That day after Yom Kippur, when Sevek made fun of my wanting to be like David and mentioned his fight with Goliath, I was insulted. First of all, it isn't my fault that King David was a redhead too. And second, I didn't mean to boast about heroism. I proposed that when Stashek came to break up our holiday we should take action together, five against one. Sevek made me look ridiculous, and none of you got up to defend me. I was insulted and went back home. The next day I still felt hurt, so I didn't go down to the yard. As I sat there at home, alone and sad, I remembered what you'd said, Sevek, and I asked myself why I didn't try to do as David had done.

"I took the Book of Samuel and reread the chapter that tells about David's exploits in the Valley of Elah. Remember? Saul said to David, 'You are not able to go up against this Philistine to fight with him; for you are but a youth, and he has been a man of war from his youth.' And David answered him: 'Your servant has killed both lions and bears.' And then, 'David put his hand in his bag and took out a stone, and slung it, and struck the Philistine on the forehead.' I said to myself, *It's true that I, Shimek, haven't killed lions or bears, but what's to stop me from practicing my aim with a slingshot?*

"That very day I made myself a slingshot. I found a gnarled branch that was split in two at the tip. I fitted two strong rubber bands to its prongs and tied them with strips of leather. There was no shortage of stones. After that you didn't see me in the yard. I was in the park. I went there every day, practicing my aim on trees and benches.

"At first I invariably missed, and my failure was a cause for despair. After all, I'm good with a bow and arrow. I'm the champion archer in our yard, and now the slingshot betrayed me! But the more I practiced, the better I got. After a week I could hit the target every time. Once a bird flew overhead. Without thinking, I aimed the slingshot and hit it as it flew. The bird dropped like a stone among the bushes. My heart ached with regret. What had I done? I never wanted to kill it!

"The accuracy of that shot encouraged me. I knew I wouldn't back down anymore. With that slingshot in my hand I would go out and hit Stashek and put an end to our disgrace.

"I planned everything down to the last detail. First I looked for a nearby spot from which I could shoot at Stashek without his noticing me. I found what I was looking for right away. I would take my post on the opposite staircase, since its window faced Stashek's window. One problem still bothered me. If Stashek actually was hit in the forehead, he'd break into the sukkah; when he saw I was not there he'd know that I was the one who shot at him, and he'd take his revenge on me. How could I cover for myself? How could I prove I was somewhere else at the time of the crime? That was when it occurred to me to get sick. A few days before the holiday I would pretend to be sick and lie in bed, and no one would be able to blame me for what happened."

"You weren't pretending!" Kubah interrupted Shimek's story. "Your mother told us you had a high temperature!"

"Right, that's what she thought," said Shimek. "At first I complained of a headache. The doctor came and couldn't find anything wrong with me. Since I was afraid of arousing suspicions, I made use of the thermometer. When my mother stuck it in my mouth I pulled a blanket over me, took out the thermometer, and rubbed it hard with my fingers. The mercury rose, and Mother believed that I really had a temperature.

"On the eve of Sukkoth I lay in bed with my slingshot and store of pebbles ready under my pillow. My heart pounded. I told my mother I wanted to go to sleep, and she closed the door to my room. Since we live on the ground floor, I opened the window and jumped out and ran barefoot to my firing position, the staircase window."

Shimek grew silent a minute, as if reflecting on that night. Then he went on.

"I crouched beneath the windowsill and fixed my eyes on the opposite window. The full moon lit up the yard, and in its light Stashek's window blackened like a dark square. When that rat's head appeared in the middle of the square, I got up, aimed my slingshot at his forehead, struggled to steady my hands, and shot the stone. When I heard Stashek scream, I knew I'd hit him on the forehead, so I slipped out of the staircase and went back to bed.

"At first I trembled all over. But afterwards I heard the holiday songs rising from the sukkah, and my heart leaped with joy. At midnight Father returned. I heard him talking with Mother in a very excited voice. It was only the next morning that I learned the truth. Father told me that the cat scratched Stashek. He was startled and fell, and in falling he hit his head. He had a brain concussion, and his life was in danger.

"I was horrified. God in Heaven! What had I done?

"Then I had no more need of tricks, such as rubbing the thermometer. I really was sick. I lay there delirious with fever.

"And that's the end of the story," Shimek said. "I decided to keep it a secret. But each day the secret weighed me down more and more, until just now when I decided to reveal it to you. After all, we've been friends for years. Even then, as I stood at the staircase window aiming the slingshot at Stashek's forehead, I sensed that I wasn't alone. That you were at my side. That my revenge on Stashek was yours too. Though I never thought the revenge would be so terrible."

And at this point Shimek covered his face in his hands and burst into tears.

We sat there stunned. We saw Shimek's shoulders quivering but we were unable to comfort him. Then Sevek got up, went over to Shimek, and embraced him.

"Shimek," he said, "it's good you told us. Now you won't have to bear the secret alone anymore. There are five of us, and it's always easier together."

Seeing that Shimek still covered his face, Sevek removed his hands by force and exclaimed, "Well, David of mine, the Bible says, 'He was ruddy and had beautiful eyes.' Stop crying! Show us your beautiful eyes!"

Sevek's words freed us from our gloom. We got up and embraced Shimek, and as he stood among us his red hair was bright as a flame and his eyes, wet with tears, were ablaze.

EDEK PAYS HIS DEBT

Who said our yard was sad?

True, closed in as it was by old, gray buildings, the yard resembled a prison. The speck of sky overhead was wrapped in smoke, which rose from the chimneys. During the day the sun put in an appearance for a little while; seemingly alarmed at what it saw, it moved on again quickly. Our fathers, who were poor, were always in a hurry as they passed through the yard, their faces heavy with gloom, as if they were pursuing something that could never be attained. But even so—

There were children in the yard, and, as children would, they played games. In the afternoons, when the boys and girls returned from school, the yard would resound with a merry, lively uproar, and laughing voices of mischief would ring out and rap on the impervious walls.

There were other pleasures too. At times a wandering beggar would appear in the yard, playing gay melodies on a squeaky music box. Hearing the tune, the tenants of the yard would open their windows, stick out their heads, and listen. After the last note quieted, the tenants would throw pennies wrapped in pieces of paper to the organ grinder, who would pick them up and put them in his pocket.

Those were the first concerts we heard.

At times a great fanfare entered our yard, announcing the arrival of a puppet show. The company would put up a booth made of curtains, and as we assembled gaping at it, puppets would appear above the booth's partition. They spoke, sang, and even quarreled and exchanged ringing blows, much to our delight. We knew that the puppets were only gloves controlled by the fingers of the person wearing them, and the voices belonged to the members of the company, but this did nothing to spoil our enjoyment. We followed the drama breathlessly.

That was the first theater we saw.

But the greatest of all were the acrobats. True, their appearances in the yard were rare, but their show was accompanied by cries of admiration and cheers. There were three of them. One played a harmonica. The second young man, a brawny fellow, took his coat off and stood there in a striped polo shirt, with blue tattoos on his muscular arms. He was assisted by a young girl barely out of childhood, pale with her hair bound in a braid as fair as flax. She too wore a polo shirt. The two of them spread a faded carpet on the stone pavement of the yard. The man clapped his hands, sprang up, turned two somersaults in the air, and landed on his feet. As we watched in admiration, he quickly stood on his hands and the wisp of a girl leaped up onto his feet. The man propelled her with a kick, and she soared like a rubber ball, only to land with her feet fixed firmly on his again. Then she sat on the ground, spreading her legs in a split or folding them behind her neck and hopping on her hands like some enormous, grotesque insect. The young man put down a little suitcase and the girl folded up her arms and legs, squeezed herself in, and was wondrously swallowed up inside the suitcase!

But that was just the beginning. Once the girl had jumped out of the suitcase and bowed to the audience, the young man led off the main act. He tied a rope high up between two posts and walked on it overhead, holding a long pole in his hands. At times he would advance on one foot alone. As the harmonica player quickened his tempo, the man on the rope would dance, hopping and spinning about, stepping back and forth, and even going head over heels to stand there upside down as the onlookers cheered him loudly.

The acrobat jumped down from the rope and the girl removed various articles from a wooden box and handed them to her partner: swords, which the man stuck in his throat up to the hilt, and all sorts of torches, which he would ignite and thrust into his mouth, swallowing the flames. The finale was the highlight of the show. The girl produced a jar of water with frogs in it, and the man took them out one after the other, set them on his outstretched hand, and popped them straight into his mouth. One, two, three frogs! The audience watched in amazement. The man's mouth was empty! Could he actually have swallowed the frogs? A minute later the performer clapped, put out his hand, and called the frogs, each one by name, and one after the other they jumped out of his mouth and returned to the jar!

The adults looked down open-mouthed from the windows. We children crowded about, excited and joyful. We didn't believe they were just acrobats—they were sorcerers!

That was the first circus we saw.

The acrobats' visit thrilled the children of the yard. We envied their agility and their tricks. For many days we discussed what we had seen. Sevek, the leader of the group, insisted that their tricks weren't the result of magic but simply practice.

"If we practice," said Sevek, "we too will be able to stand on our heads, walk a tightrope, or fold up and squeeze into a suitcase."

"But what about swallowing the fire and the swords and the frogs?" asked Kubah. Sevek, who was skeptical by nature, had an explanation for that too.

"Perhaps," he said, "they weren't real swords but just fakes. A sword like that can be folded up to the hilt, and it looks to the audience as if it's stuck in the throat."

"And the fire?"

"It's a cold fire," asserted Sevek. "I read once that you could make a fire like that."

"And the frogs?" argued Shimek. "We saw him swallow them with our own eyes!"

"That's just sleight of hand," replied Sevek. "Maybe the frogs jumped into his sleeve."

"But there weren't any sleeves on his polo shirt!" I argued.

"Then they stayed there in his hand," replied Sevek. "It's just a matter of practice."

We were angry with Sevek for having broken the spell that enchanted us, but deep in our hearts we had to admit that he was right.

Edek was the only one not to give up. "If it was all just a matter of practice and sleight of hand, why shouldn't we try to copy them?" he asked.

"First of all," said Sevek, "we don't have the money to buy the necessary equipment—collapsible swords and cold fire. As for frogs, they make me sick. I'd vomit if I had to hold one of them in my hand."

"And the stunts on the tightrope?" Edek persisted.

"I don't have a mind to run any risks," replied Sevek. "I'd probably fall and break my neck."

Edek wasn't convinced. He seemed to take Sevek's word regarding the swords, fire, and frogs, but the idea of the rope stuck in his mind.

A week later, as we went out to the back yard, we caught our breath in surprise. A thick rope extended from the hinge of one of the stockroom doors to the hinge of the opposite door. Edek hung in midair, gripping the rope in his hands, which he advanced one after the other to move forward, high above the yard. At the halfway point he stopped and swung his legs like two pendulums. Beginning slowly he quickened their swing and suddenly threw his whole body in a tremendous somersault and turned over in space, while gripping the rope in his hands. Then he jumped down and stood before us with a victorious smile on his face. "Where did you learn that?" we asked in astonishment.

"I've been practicing here every day," replied Edek. "You, Sevek, protested that you'd break your neck in practice. But I tried and succeeded!"

From then on we had no need of performing acrobats. Every day we witnessed all kinds of shows. One time Edek tied his rope to the top of the chestnut tree and climbed it, hand over hand, with his legs gripping the rope between them. Another time he stretched the rope very high above the back yard and moved forward across it on his back like a chameleon, holding onto the rope with his hands and ankles. We stood there in admiration and fear. What would happen if, Heaven forbid, he should lose his grip for a minute?

But Edek didn't let go. Through practice he had reached perfection. He was quick as a monkey, and a professional acrobat would have been proud of his stunts.

Edek was rewarded with cheers and adoration, but his tricks brought him trouble too. Several times his father, Mendel the grocer, who stored his vegetables in the back yard, happened to pass by. At the sight of his son dangling on a rope between earth and sky, he shouted so loudly that we were afraid Edek would be frightened and fall. But Edek got down safely somehow or other. Once he set foot on the ground he was greeted with a slap on the cheek, as his father assailed him angrily.

"Are you crazy? What's a Jewish boy doing clowning around like an acrobat? I send you to school to study and learn, and you go climbing ropes like a worthless fool!"

But the slaps that were Edek's lot from time to time did not rid him of his yearning for the rope. He continued to practice, filling every free hour with his breathtaking tricks and stunts. We all loved to play, but when Edek took up with a game it was as if the devil were in him. He played devotedly, passionately, until he was numb with excitement.

But there came a day when Edek stopped playing. He abandoned the rope and he abandoned us too, his friends.

Kubah's little brother, a boy of six, had an accident. His name was Mordechai, but everyone called him Moti. Moti followed Kubah around and followed us too, bothering us as we played. We ordered him more than once to leave the yard. When we did, Moti would run home crying.

One day we heard screams. A wagon loaded with boxes drove into the back yard and little Moti dashed straight at the horse's hooves and was trampled. Both legs were severely injured, and he had to be taken to the hospital. I can still hear his mother screaming as Moti was pulled out from beneath the wagon wheels. I can still see his father, Nathan the tailor, a squat, humpbacked Jew, leaning against the wall and wringing his hands, his lips quivering. Moti's injury saddened the children in the yard, but it was Edek who was shocked the most. After the accident he stopped playing with us. He left the group and went around with a gloomy look. Several times we saw him sitting under the chestnut tree, his head bent, an image of sadness and dejection.

"What happened to you, Edek?" we asked.

At first he was silent. Though we repeatedly urged him, he kept still. A week later, however, as we sat on the broad wooden stoop of one of the stockrooms in the back yard, Edek appeared and stood before us. A sorrowful expression was on his face. We wanted to question him, but Edek beat us to it and said, "I'm to blame for Moti's accident. If I hadn't chased him, he wouldn't have been run over."

Seeing our looks of astonishment, Edek went on with his confession.

"That day I took my rope and went out to practice. There wasn't a soul in the yard. Suddenly Moti appeared, snatched the rope from my hand, and fled to a corner of the yard. 'Give it back this minute!' I shouted, and when he didn't obey me I threatened to hit him. Moti panicked and started running for the gate, with me behind him. And then—then the wagon came and . . ."

Edek burst into tears as we sat there, stunned and silent. We wanted to console him, but the tormented look on his face left our throats choked. Finally Sevek said, "You're torturing yourself for nothing, Edek. After all, how could you know that Moti would be run over when he fled from you?"

But Edek went on sobbing. "I'm to blame!" he cried. "All my life I'll be in debt to Moti!"

We gave Edek our word we'd keep his secret and never reveal it to anyone. But Edek wasn't comforted. He left us, a sorrowful expression on his face, his eyes red with tears.

Moti spent a month in the hospital. All that time Edek kept his distance from us and never joined our games. One day Moti was brought back home with both his legs in casts. Naturally, we paid him a visit. Moti had not said a word about the circumstances that led to his injury. It must have been that the shock he'd suffered in falling beneath the horse's hooves had wiped the memory of the rope from his mind.

We called on Moti only once, but Edek visited him every day. He sat with Moti for hours, reading him stories, drawing pictures for him, playing checkers and dominoes with him. On his visits Edek would bring whatever he could take on the sly from his father's grocery: a tasty pear, an apple, a bag of almonds or raisins. At times he even lifted an orange—a rare fruit in our parts—or a bar of chocolate. He neglected his homework and spent most of his time at Moti's bedside. At the sight of the boy's little legs in their casts, his remorse was renewed continually. Moti's mother and humpbacked father would praise Edek and tell the neighbors, "That boy has a heart of gold!"

Days and weeks passed. Little by little Moti got over the shock. His memory returned. One evening as he lay alone in his room, leafing through a picture book, a gift from Edek, his gaze came to rest on a coil of rope that his mother had left on the table. All at once his memory of the scene returned. He saw himself fleeing for his life with the rope, Edek in pursuit. He shut his eyes, but the horrifying image of the horse's hooves rising above him did not disappear. Moti buried his face in his pillow and wept. At once his mother and father burst into the room.

"What happened to you, Moti? Why are you crying?"

Sobbing loudly, Moti told his parents that Edek had chased him on the day of the accident, and it was his fault that he had been run over.

The next day, Edek showed up at Moti's house as usual. This time he had decided to surprise the boy. He would bring him his most precious possession as a gift. Edek had a broken spyglass with no lenses, which he played with all the time. He used it to keep watch from the uppermost branches and imagine he was a sailor in the crow's nest, searching for land. Now he offered Moti the spyglass and said, "Take it. It's for you."

Moti grabbed the spyglass, flung it down, and shouted, "I don't need your presents! You're to blame for everything! You chased me, and it was your fault I was run over. I don't want to see your face! Take your spyglass and leave me alone!" Moti began wailing loudly.

Edek stood there, his face pale, his whole body shaking. He wanted to say something, to explain, to justify himself, but he couldn't make a sound. Just then Moti's father entered the room. He had come up by chance from his store when his son's wailing alarmed him. At the sight of Edek, the humpback's face grew crimson, and he charged at him with both fists clenched.

"Don't you dare come here, you sneak!" screamed Nathan. "Moti told us everything."

"But—" Edek stammered. "It wasn't my fault. We were playing in the yard and Moti ran and didn't notice the wagon. I—"

Moti's father cut him short. "Shut up, you murderer! Get out!"

Humiliated, Edek fled. In Edek's mind Nathan the humpback was pursuing him. In another minute he'd catch up with him and pummel him with his fists. His heart pounded as he returned home and shut himself in his room. A little while later he was startled by angry voices rising from the yard. He went up to the window, where his eyes beheld the figure of his father, Mendel, who was leaning against the wall with his arms outstretched in defense. Nathan the humpback was facing him and yelling in a high, piercing voice.

"No, I won't keep quiet! I'll make him pay, that hoodlum of yours! I'll turn him in to the police!"

Edek withdrew from the window, dropped on his bed, and buried his face in the pillow. Later he felt a hand on his head. His father stood beside him, his sad eyes looking at him without a word.

"Father," Edek burst into tears, "I'm not to blame!" Edek told his father how it had come about that day in the back yard. His father listened to his story and patted his head.

"Son," he said, "don't torment yourself. After all, you didn't mean any harm to Moti."

"I know that," replied Edek, who had stopped crying. "But what can I do, Father? I haven't had a peaceful moment since then. I have the feeling that I'm terribly in debt to Moti and I'll never be able to pay him back!"

The next day the tenants in the yard were jolted out of their tranquility. At noon there was a scream of terror.

"Fire!"

We all dashed out to the yard—old men, women, and children. Black, thick smoke rose from Nathan the humpback's window on the third floor. In the window little Moti's head was visible as he reached out and shrieked, "Help!"

We learned later that Moti, who was left alone in the house, had been playing with matches. A burning match had fallen from his hand, and the fire took hold of the straw mat that extended from his room to the hall. There, by the front door, a can of kerosene caught fire. Without the casts on his legs, Moti might have been able to crawl out and save himself, but the fire in the hall blocked his way. The boy was caught in a trap of flames. He climbed a chair and stood at the window screaming, the fear of death on his face.

A few neighbors ran up to the third floor. The door was ablaze. The hall was burning like a gigantic torch. There was no chance of breaking into the apartment.

Meanwhile, the screaming in the yard increased. Moti's mother's voice was the loudest as she tore her hair, beat her head against the wall, and shrieked, "Save my son!"

People ran this way and that, confounded. Some rushed to sound the fire alarm; others took pillows and quilts and piled them up on the stone pavement beneath the window. One neighbor brought a blanket, and four young men held it by the corners and pulled tight.

"They've called the fire department!" someone protested.

"They won't get here on time. The whole apartment will be on fire by then!"

They called up to Moti, who was standing at the window. "Jump, Moti, we'll catch you! Nothing will happen to you!"

But Moti burst into tears and cried, "I'm scared!"

Pillars of smoke surrounded his little form, while behind him, in the background, great flames flickered.

Watching from the crowd below, my whole body shook from fright. All at once I caught sight of something moving on the roof. I looked and held my breath.

On the height of the sloping roof, above the fourth story, Edek appeared with a rope in his hand, the rope he had abandoned since Moti's accident. Edek crawled along the roof, looped one end of the rope around the red brick chimney, and tied a knot in it. Then he gripped it in both hands and slid down the slope to the edge of the roof.

The people in the yard saw what was happening, and they were instantly silent. There was an intense, terrible hush, with only Moti's voice, broken and sobbing, calling, "Help!"

Suddenly Mendel, Edek's father, shouted, "Edek, come back! Do you hear? Don't you dare!"

Edek paid no attention to the warning. He let his legs dangle over the eaves and eased himself down the rope to the third-floor window.

We all held our breath. Now he was descending, gripping the rope with his hands and legs, and his body, hanging in space, blocked the window and hid Moti from us.

"Moti!" Edek shouted. "Get on my back!"

Moti hesitated. Then he put out his two little hands and clutched Edek's neck. In another minute he was clinging to his back like a sack of potatoes.

Edek turned around in midair, faced the wall of the building, and began his descent. One minute he tightened the rope between his feet; the next minute he let it go, planted his feet on the wall, and walked on it as if it were level ground. All the while his hands gripped the rope desperately. One hand let go for an instant and slid down, and then the other joined it in its descent. Lower and lower, bit by bit, the second floor, the first . . .

Close to the ground, about a yard and a half above the pavement, Edek's muscles gave out. The burden on his back was too much for him. He let go of the rope and both of them, Moti and Edek, fell and landed on the taut blanket. Edek jumped down on the stone pavement, safe. Moti, because of the casts on his legs, still lay on the blanket, unharmed.

Then the silence burst like a balloon. The yard was filled with the din of excited voices. Moti's mother dashed over to him and covered his face with kisses. His father, Nathan the squat humpback, went up to Edek's father, embraced him, propped his head on his chest, and burst into tears like a little boy.

Just then the sound of a trumpet came from the street. The fire chief appeared in the yard, riding a white horse and wearing a shiny copper helmet. The firemen unrolled their hoses, climbed up their ladders, which reached up to the window engulfed in smoke, and poured jets of water into the apartment. We, the fellows in the group, who had always been thrilled by the sight of firemen at their job, were indifferent to them this time. We surrounded Edek, who stood there winding the rope on his arm. His eyes lowered, and a smile played about his mouth. It was his first smile since that summer day when Moti was run over.

We smiled too. And we were silent. There was nothing to say.

QUEEN OF THE YARD

The second-story apartment, vacated when its tenants moved to the next block, was occupied again. One day, returning from school, I saw a huge, two-horse van and porters unloading tables, chairs, and boxes packed with household articles. The newcomers who had arrived to take up residence in our yard were a family of three: the father, a tall Jew, his face framed in a coal-black beard; the mother, a short, thin woman; and the daughter, a green-eyed, pug-nosed girl, whose brown hair was plaited in two thick braids. Her name was Rachel, but her parents called her Ulah. We, the boys in the yard, preferred the nickname.

Ulah was fourteen years old, the same age as Sevek. She lent her parents a hand taking their things up to the new apartment. As she moved, her braids danced on her back. We observed her curiously while she, it seemed, ignored us. Once or twice she stole a glance in our direction.

The next day, in the afternoon, we went out as usual to play in the yard, which was our soccer field. The ball, a sock filled with dirt, went flying every which way. Our attempts to score a goal were in vain. Sevek defended the goalposts with a passion, hopping and pouncing and flinging himself down to block the heavy ball, which banged into him with a dull thud.

As we were kicking the ball around, caught up in the game, Ulah appeared in the yard. She wore pants, and her long braids were tied at the back of her neck. Before we could say anything to stop her, Ulah kicked the ball, which flew up in a wide arc and landed next to the goal. Sevek was taken aback at first, but then he went up to Ulah.

"Don't interfere," he said. "This isn't a game for girls."

"Who asked you?" retorted Ulah. Her green eyes flashed a teasing glance at Sevek.

They both stood there a moment, sizing each other up. Sevek lowered his eyes first and said, "Go away."

Ulah did not go away. She stayed in the yard. Every once in a while, when the ball landed near her, she kicked it. We boys were forced to put up with her presence. Ulah's manner made it clear that the only way to get rid of her would be by force, but we had always abided by the unwritten law: *Boys should never lift a hand to girls.*

We went on with the game. Edek repeatedly passed to Kubah, who broke out and kicked the ball at the goal, but Sevek blocked it every time.

Suddenly the ball landed in the middle of the yard. Ulah, who was standing on the sidelines, rushed at it and aimed it at the goal with a powerful kick. Sevek sprang forward but missed it. A goal!

I stood nearby and watched Sevek's face. He turned a little pale, and his lips tightened.

"That's all. The game's over!" Sevek announced, and he took the ball and was gone. We too left the yard. I turned back to glance at Ulah. She stood there somewhat puzzled, but her green eyes sparkled.

The next day we went to the park to play. Sevek announced, "Okay, gang, let's have a race!"

We climbed to the top of the hill, the slope of which served as our track. Just then Ulah appeared at our side. Sevek, crouching to the ground and marking off our starting line with a stick, was the last to notice her. He stood up, went over to her, and snapped, "What are you following us around for? Go play dolls with your girl friends."

Ulah stood straight, unawed, her height no less than his. Her green eyes flamed back at his black eyes of resentment.

"This hill is mine as much as yours," she said.

"I order you not to race!" Sevek yelled.

"I couldn't care less about your orders," retorted Ulah. "You can tell your little playmates what to do and they'll obey you like slaves. I, for the time being, have no lord and master."

Sevek held his tongue, weighing his words. At last he said slowly, driving every word home, "Look, Ulah, I told you to go away for your own good. We just never play with girls."

"May I know why not?" asked Ulah.

"Because they don't know how to play like us," replied Sevek, "even though you did score a goal against me yesterday, by accident. But racing is no sport for girls."

"Are you sure?" Ulah asked.

Sevek seemed ready to reply but threw up his hands in exasperation. "Okay," he said, "I can see you're a stubborn one. Go on and race. There's enough room for us all. What do I care if you bring up the rear?"

We found our places on the starting line, Sevek, Shimek, Kubah, Edek, and I. Quickly Ulah stooped, picked up a stick, and scratched a mark on the ground, lengthening the starting line. Then she took her place there, several paces from us.

"Ready!" cried Sevek, taking no notice of Ulah. "Get set! Go!"

We sprang forward. At our side, in her lane, Ulah raced, her long braids flying behind her.

We were good runners, but Sevek was the fastest. At the halfway mark he passed us, his head thrust forward as if ready to ram any obstacles he might encounter.

Just then, as we ran, we saw Ulah moving up in her lane! She drew closer to Sevek and overtook him. For a minute they ran neck and neck, but as they advanced Ulah put on speed. She passed Sevek, dashed out in front, and was the first to cross the finish line at the bottom of the hill.

Sevek finished second, panting and sweaty and scowling. We stood about, peering at them speechlessly. It was our amazement that struck us dumb. Sevek, however, was choked with anger. Finally he exploded.

"Go away! Don't you dare follow us around anymore! Do you understand?"

Ulah shrugged, chastened, her lips trembling. Then she stood up straight and rapped out a single word.

"Loudmouth!"

"What did you say?" shouted Sevek, red-faced.

Ulah hesitated a minute and then repeated it, in a clearer voice this time.

"Loudmouth!"

That's when it happened. Sevek broke the unwritten law. He charged head forward and rammed into Ulah's chest.

It was a hard blow. Ulah swayed. We were sure she would fall, but she remained standing, very pale, and hissed, "So that's what you want? A fight? Fine!"

She promptly threw a punch at Sevek's jaw. Sevek ducked, but not fast enough. Ulah's fist caught him in the forehead.

Sevek took the blow. We still believed he would restrain himself, but blind with rage and humiliation, he sprang at Ulah. In a minute, they were rolling on the ground.

We stood there watching the spectacle, excited and distraught.

"Sevek!" we yelled. "Are you out of your mind? Leave her alone!"

We wanted to break it up, to save Sevek from disgrace. We had always felt it was a point of honor not to lift a hand to a girl. But something stopped us. Our pride, a boy's pride, had been wounded. How could that girl dare challenge Sevek? She had humiliated all of us. True, it was Sevek who had started the fight and violated the sacred code, but the law had been broken by Ulah. It was she who had followed us around. So let her have a taste of Sevek's punishment. He'd teach her to do what she was told!

They rolled on the ground, grappling fiercely. One minute it seemed Sevek was winning, and the next it seemed Ulah was on top. Sevek fought wildly. Snatching Ulah's hand and twisting it behind her, he grabbed her waist with his other hand and bore down upon her. Ulah, agile as a cat, managed to slip out of his grip. A minute later she was astride him, sinking her elbows into his chest and pinning his back to the ground.

We stood in a ring, holding our breath. The scales were turning. We heard Sevek gasping and Ulah panting. All at once, Ulah wound an arm through Sevek's arms from behind. Linking her fingers, she pressed her locked hands on the back of his neck and bent his head steadily down.

The battle was won. Ulah had made use of the hold we knew from Tarzan movies. There was no chance of Sevek's breaking out of her full nelson.

Sevek sprawled on his belly with Ulah crouching over him, pushing his face in the dust. They squirmed another minute, twisting convulsively, but in the end they were still.

Sevek was beaten. Ulah loosened her hold on him, jumped up, and ran away from us fast. Sevek was still stretched out on the ground. After a while he sat up with an icy, expressionless look on his face. He rose slowly, shaking the dirt from his clothes.

We walked home in silence, our heads down. We were afraid to look Sevek in the eye.

Sevek was humbled. For years we all accepted his authority. Suddenly a tall, green-eyed girl appeared and made him crawl, rubbing his nose in the dirt. After Ulah's triumph Sevek became gloomy and silent.

At first our hearts were with Sevek. His disgrace was ours. But little by little our sympathy for him lessened. The first to break away was Shimek the redhead, who had always envied Sevek and wanted to claim the leader's crown for his own.

"Did you see Sevek?" Shimek said to me one day. "The way he goes around hanging his head? To tell you the truth, I'm not sorry he lost. He thought he was our boss. I'm glad Ulah taught him a lesson."

I was hurt by what Shimek said. I protested. "Rejoice not when thine enemy falleth," I quoted.

"Sevek isn't my enemy," replied Shimek. "It's just that I always had a feeling we were letting him dominate us."

"He's older than we are," I argued.

"So what?" cried Shimek. "Ulah is too. She's the same age he is."

"So what's preventing you from going along with her?" I asked.

"Don't forget she's a girl. I'll never take orders from a girl."

Shimek didn't keep his word. That very day I saw Ulah playing in the yard, tossing a red rubber ball in the air and catching it. When the ball fell, Shimek ran after it, picked it up, and brought it back to Ulah.

Soon enough Kubah joined them, becoming another one of Ulah's tools. Thus we split into two rival camps: Ulah, Shimek, and Kubah versus Sevek, Edek, and me. As time passed, relations between us worsened. Before long we were enemies.

Every day after school, Ulah would appear in the yard, wearing a T-shirt and sneakers. The minute she whistled, Shimek and Kubah would present themselves, and the three of them would begin a game in the yard. Then Sevek would beckon to Edek and me, and we would set off for the park. Sometimes we'd reach the park and encounter Ulah and her followers. When we did, we returned to the yard. It seemed there wasn't enough room for all of us in one place.

Ulah was pretty. She had a way with everyone. It was no wonder the tenants liked her. Even Antony, the drunken Polish doorman, used to welcome her, saying, "How are you, my beauty?" Stashek, his adopted son, tried to take up with her at first, but Ulah shook him off, driving him away like an annoying fly. Stashek let her go, but every time he came across her he would give her a broad, obsequious smile.

It was hard to resist Ulah's charms. One day when I went out to the yard with Sevek, we discovered Edek playing hopscotch with Ulah. Now Edek was a deserter too. Sevek kept still, but I felt my blood boil. I couldn't control myself. I shook my fist and cried, "Traitor!"

Edek glanced at us, blushing, but then he quickly went back, lowered his head, and resumed the game.

Ulah stood aside, gazing at us with her eyes wide open. Suddenly she left Edek and began striding toward Sevek. An embarrassed little smile played about her lips.

My heart stopped. Could it be true? Ulah's smile left no room for doubt. In another minute she'd offer her hand in peace. But Sevek started as if bitten by a snake, and he ran out of the yard. I ran after him.

The next day I went to visit Sevek. He was sitting by the window, peeking out. After a while Ulah appeared in the yard, her two brown braids wound around her head like a crown. Sevek never took his eyes off her. Then I heard him whisper, "That's the Queen of the Yard!"

I thought he'd elaborate and call her a name. But Sevek said nothing more.

"Let's go play in the park," I suggested.

Sevek made no reply. As if nailed to the spot, he sat by the window and followed Ulah with his eyes.

I looked at her too, reluctantly admiring her every movement. First she sent the red ball flying. Then she was jumping rope. Then skipping quickly. Her body was lithe as a spring.

The more I looked at Ulah the more I reproached myself. Was there really no way out of the contention between us? My heart was drawn to the yard, but I remained with Sevek, talking to myself.

"You too, Benny?"

"Yes, me too."

"Then why don't you join up with her?"

"I'll never betray Sevek. And he hates her. He hates her like poison."

"Really?"

The last question was prompted by Sevek's appearance as he bent over the window, careful not to let his head stick out. His eyes gazed sadly and longingly at the scene before him. Sitting there without moving a muscle, Sevek suddenly cupped his face in his hands and propped his head on the windowsill.

I slipped out. That night I went to bed early. The dusk of evening descended slowly. Shadows cloaked the room. I peered at the darkness creeping out of the corners, and Ulah's image appeared before me. As I looked at the Queen of the Yard all at once I saw Sevek, his head on the windowsill and his shoulders shaking, and my heart ached with pity for my tortured friend.

The next day I sat by the gate, watching Ulah as she played soccer with Shimek, Kubah, and Edek. From my seat I had a good view of her face. She played a hard game, but every so often she stole a shy, hopeful glance at Sevek's window. I glanced up. Sevek sat there in the shadow of the curtain, looking out at the yard.

Suddenly Ulah kicked the ball. It soared and smashed into Antony the doorman's window. The pane was shattered. Ulah, Shimek, Kubah, and Edek fled for their lives. So did I, running to the staircase, where I peeked through a window to see what would happen next.

Antony stormed out of his cellar apartment, his drunkard's face flaming.

"Who did it?" he screamed, his voice quivering with rage. Antony stood there in the yard, ready to charge and avenge himself on the first victim he could find.

I heard steps from the opposite staircase. Sevek appeared in the yard and made straight for Antony.

"I broke the window," Sevek said. "I didn't mean to. The ball . . ."

He didn't get to finish the sentence. Antony took him by the scruff of his neck and made a fist with his other hand, raining blows on Sevek.

"You scamp, you good-for-nothing, you hooligan!" screamed Antony.

Sevek put up his hands, shielding his face from the blows. Antony's fist pummeled his body, but Sevek never made a sound.

Just then Ulah burst into the yard. She grabbed Antony's fist and hung onto his arm.

"Please, Mr. Antony," she implored him, "don't beat Sevek. He's not to blame. We'll raise the money and pay you back."

Antony froze and gazed at Ulah.

"Well, my beauty, who can resist you?" he said, and let Sevek go.

Ulah wound her arm about Sevek's waist and led him to her house. With her other hand she stroked his head, which was resting on her shoulder.

"Did you see that?" asked Shimek, coming out with the other boys. His eyes were wide with amazement.

Kubah was bewildered too. "Who would ever have believed it?" he exclaimed.

Edek said nothing.

From then on our gang was without a leader. Sevek's reign of glory had passed, and Ulah's, which rose so quickly, faded now as well.

Sevek and Ulah left the group. In the evenings, when our parents called us in to supper, we would see them sitting in the yard, leaning on the trunk of the chestnut tree and whispering together. They were older than we were and had secrets of their own. We didn't hold it against them.

JB

Tene, Benjamin
In the shade of the chestnut
tree

copy 1

DATE DUE			
11/17/81			

Temple Beth-El Library
Great Neck, N. Y.